Big Loss or Big Gain?

Lucky remembered what Romaine had done when they ran the play earlier. He started to the right and watched for the pitch. It came a little hard, however, and in front of him. Lucky reached out and tipped the ball high in the air. He was able to run under it and catch it — almost. Just as he was about to take off with the football, the thing somehow slithered through his arms, down his body, and onto the grass. He stopped, picked it up, dropped it, picked it up again, and then looked up to see two tacklers coming hard from the right side.

BOOKS BY DEAN HUGHES

From Deseret Book

The Lucky books
Lucky's Crash Landing
Lucky Breaks Loose
Lucky's Gold Mine

The Williams family historical novels
Under the Same Stars
As Wide as the River
Facing the Enemy
Cornbread and Prayer

Other titles
Brothers
Hooper Haller
Jenny Haller
The Mormon Church, a Basic History

From other publishers

The Nutty books
Nutty for President
Nutty and the Case of the Mastermind Thief
Nutty and the Case of the Ski-Slope Spy
Nutty Can't Miss
Nutty Knows All
Nutty, the Movie Star

The Angel Park All-Stars
Making the Team
Big Base Hit

Other titles
Jelly's Circus
Family Pose *(released in
paperback as* Family Picture*)*

LUCKY
BREAKS LOOSE

DEAN HUGHES

CINNAMON
TREE™

Published by
Deseret Book Company
Salt Lake City, Utah

For Jim and Susan Waite

©1990 Dean Hughes

All rights reserved. No part of this book may be reproduced in any form or by any means without permission in writing from the publisher, Deseret Book Company, P.O. Box 30178, Salt Lake City, Utah 84130.

Deseret Book is a registered trademark of Deseret Book Company.

Library of Congress Cataloging-in-Publication Data

Hughes, Dean, 1943–
Lucky breaks loose / by Dean Hughes.
   p. cm.
Summary: Lucky's attempts to befriend a black football player at his new school help him break through racial barriers.
   ISBN 0-87579-194-8
    [1. Race relations—Fiction. 2. Prejudices—Fiction.
3. Friendship—Fiction. 4. Football—Fiction. 5. Schools—
Fiction.]   I. Title.
PZ7.H87312Lu 1990
[Fic]—dc20
                                    90-30850
                                         CIP
                                         AC

Printed in the United States of America
10   9   8   7   6   5   4   3   2   1

CHAPTER 1

"**H**ey, wait up!" Lucky yelled, but Malcolm didn't look back, didn't even slow down. Lucky had to run to get his shorter legs going fast enough to make up ground on Malcolm's long ones. "Can I talk to you a minute?"

Malcolm kept right on walking. "What about?"

Lucky jogged to stay up. "I was just thinking—I won't be around too long, but if you want to be friends we could—"

Malcolm stopped. "No, thanks," he said.

"Why not? Don't you—"

"I can't believe you asked—in front of the whole class—who the Mormons were."

Lucky shrugged. "I always do that. It's a good way to meet the Mormon kids the first day. If I wait until Sunday, I—"

"I'm not a Mormon. Not really. Some guys know

1

that's where I go to church, and that's the only reason they said that."

"Well, that doesn't matter. We could still be friends."

"I've got plenty of friends. I don't need any white ones." He started walking again.

Lucky knew he shouldn't tag along. Still, he always thought that, if he talked with someone long enough, he could work out any problem.

"What are you doing?" Malcolm said after his long strides didn't shake Lucky loose.

"You're not from here, are you? Where did you move from?"

Malcolm didn't answer at first. Finally he said, "Chicago."

"Oh, yeah? What brought you to Louisiana?"

"My dad got transferred. But look, you don't need to—"

"To little old Pascal, from Chicago?"

"He works in town, in Lafayette. We just live out here."

"Ah. That explains it. What kind of work does he do?"

Malcolm halted again. His eyes were set; his hair, blocked; and his chin, square. He seemed firm as a wall. "You're weird—you know that? You look weird and you talk weird. I don't want to talk about my dad. I want you to get lost. You got that? I got to get to football practice." Malcolm took off again; he was almost running. Lucky tried to keep up. "Football? Are you on a football team?"

Malcolm didn't answer. He cut across the street. Lucky crossed too. He tried to think what he could say to Malcolm that would break the ice. And then the sidewalk came up and slammed against his chest. Lucky took a second or two to realize what had happened. He'd been looking ahead and tripped over the curb.

Lucky rolled over and tried to get his breath. He saw little patterns—like ornamental snow-flakes—floating before his eyes.

"What happened?" Malcolm had come back.

"I tripped . . . I guess."

Malcolm looked as if he were about to say something, but he kept his mouth shut. Lucky wondered if he wasn't such a hard guy as he put on. For a moment, he had looked really concerned.

Lucky always made up his mind quickly. Right then he decided that, one way or another, he'd get to know Malcolm better. "I've got to be more careful," he said. "I could get hurt some time." He took some deep breaths. "But I'm lucky. I crash, but I don't burn." He rolled back over and got up to his knees. After testing his balance, he stood.

"I swear, you're weird." Malcolm walked away.

Lucky followed but didn't try to keep up. At the next corner, Malcolm entered a small park. Lucky saw two men wearing sweats. He figured they were the coaches. He decided to go over and watch practice at least for a few minutes.

"Hey, Struthers," one of the coaches said as Malcolm walked up, "you got here fast today. You must be ready to play."

"I am," Malcolm replied.

"Who's your buddy?"

Malcolm spun around. He obviously hadn't realized Lucky was still behind him.

"Hello," Lucky said to the coach. "I'm Lucky Ladd." He stuck his hand out. "I'm new in town."

The coach laughed. Then he shook Lucky's hand. "What's that on your shirt?" he asked.

Lucky brushed away some dust and dirt. "Oh, well, I had a little battle with the sidewalk back there. I think it won."

The coach was trim yet muscular in his chest, but he was no youngster. His crew-cut hair was thinning and graying along the sides. "I'm Bob Denton," he said. He also introduced the other coach— his son Johnny. "How come you're called Lucky?" he asked. He sounded Southern, but he didn't have the Cajun accent that Lucky had been hearing from some of the local people.

"My dad calls me that. When I was born—on the way to the hospital—we were in a bad wreck, but no one got hurt too bad. There were some broken bones and cuts, and one toe cut off, but nothing serious. And I was born pretty normal—with only a few minor adjustments needed. So Dad said I was good luck." Lucky normally gave more details to his story, but he had done that at school, and he didn't think Malcolm wanted to hear it again.

Coach Denton was laughing. "What brought you to Pascal?"

"My dad's here because of the tornado. He's an insurance man, and he has to appraise all the damage."

"Is he the one who drives a big RV parked right there by the Home and Farm insurance office on Main Street?"

"Yup. That's us. Our house is our car, and our car is our house. We move every few weeks, so that's the best way."

"What does your mom think of that kind of life?"

"My mom died last year."

The coach nodded. "That's too bad," he said. "Well, your dad will be visiting me. My house got ripped up pretty good. And I've got my insurance down at Home and Farm."

"How come you're still coaching if your house got torn up?"

He grinned. "Hey, I can't let a little wind stop me. We got us a good team this year. You going to play with us?"

Lucky was taken by surprise. "Oh. I don't know. We'll be here just two or three weeks . . . and I'm sort of . . . I mean, I've never played much football before."

"It's just flag football. There's no tackling. You grab the flags off these belt things." He held up a set of flags. "See, they're hooked on with that Velcro stuff."

"Well, I don't know. I'm not too good at sports. Except I am into skateboarding some. I guess I'm not too bad at that."

Coach Denton thought that was funny. "Skateboarding? What kind of sport is that?"

"It's a good one. Out in California guys can do all kinds of things. I can do a three-sixty—or at least two-seventy—and I was learning to jump off a ramp—'catching air,' they call it—but I wiped out and got a concussion and had to go to the hospital overnight, but still, I wasn't too bad, at least for a guy who doesn't have—you know—too much hand/eye coordination."

"Well, I think you ought to learn to play some football." He gave Lucky a big nod. "There's no sport like it."

"Coach," Malcolm said, "he doesn't have time to learn the plays. Anyway, he's so little he'll get killed."

"Well, Struthers, just about ever'body I know was little before they got big. He might as well learn what he can while he's here. That's what this whole league is about, you know."

That made sense to Lucky. "Yeah, I guess I'd like to play. I'm not sure what position, though. I don't think I could be a lineman, because, as Malcolm says, I'm a little undersized. I guess I could be a running back. I haven't played on a regular team, but I've played with a bunch of guys, and I've watched sometimes. We don't have a television in the RV, but every now and then, I've been at some guy's house when—"

"Well, listen, Lucky. Why don't you and Malcolm get a ball and throw it around a little. When the other guys get here, we'll work you in somewheres. How's that?"

Malcolm's bullet eyes seemed ready to fire, yet he didn't say anything. He pulled a football from a canvas bag. Lucky backed away to take a throw. Instead, Malcolm yelled, "Hey, Winslow," at a big kid—another black guy—coming across the park, and he threw him a pass. Winslow lumbered toward the ball, but it bounced off his chest. He was big enough to knock down three or four guys the size of Lucky.

Coach Denton saw what Malcolm had done. "Hey, Lucky," he said, "I think I *will* make you a running back. Are you fast?"

"Well, yes and no. I run fast, but my legs don't reach very far. Some guys run slower, but they get there faster."

Coach Denton laughed. "That's all right. Your flags'll be down low. It won't be easy to git hold of 'em." He stepped closer to Lucky. "You do need to get a mouthpiece for the games. If you got hit, those braces of yours would go right through your lip. You should be all right for practice today though. We're mostly running through basics."

"Okay. I'll get one." Lucky wondered, though, what he was getting into when he saw the rest of the players show up. Winslow was the biggest, but several others were close to his size.

Quite a few players had already taken off the sweats covering their shorts. Coach Denton started practice by having the boys run twice around the park. No one ran very fast, and Lucky kept up. Malcolm acted as though he didn't know Lucky was even there. He was with Winslow and two other friends: a guy named Philip, and another everyone called "Stick."

Johnny led the boys in stretching exercises and some jumping jacks. Then he had them run in place and, on signal, dive to the ground and pop back up. "That's it, Lucky," Coach Denton called out. "That's just right." Lucky figured he was lucky to be so close to the ground. The other guys had to dive from higher up.

By the time the drills were finished, Lucky was feeling the humidity. The October temperature wasn't that high, but the air was full of moisture. Lucky was dripping with perspiration. Now he understood why so many on the team had worn sweats to school but played in shorts at the park.

After drills, the coach had the boys line up in an offense and defense. "This boy is called Lucky," he said. "Lucky Ladd. Some of you got to know him at school. He isn't going to be around long, but he's going to play running back. So you other backs—I want you to help him learn what he's supposed to do."

A big guy grinned at Lucky and said, "I'll show

you what to do. When I rush Malcolm, you just try to stop me."

"He'll do that," Coach Denton said. "Lucky's a smart kid. I'll show him some tricks, and he'll put you on your back."

This got laughs, but Lucky overheard Philip say to Malcolm, "The little shrimp is going to get killed."

"That's his problem," Malcolm said. "If he had sense, he wouldn't play." Malcolm stayed close to Winslow and Philip and the other black guys. Lucky also noticed a group of Cajun boys who hung around each other. The other white guys had their group too. He wondered why they wanted to divide up that way.

The coach added some new plays, explaining how they worked. The first one was a pass. The job of the running back was to block. All he did was shuffle forward, putting his arms up in front of his chest. Lucky saw no problem. The offense ran the play several times while the defense watched. It didn't take long to see that Malcolm was one of the best athletes. He threw the ball hard with a lot more accuracy than Lucky expected from a boy in sixth grade.

"Okay, boys, let's get a defense in there. You

linemen rush hard, and let's see if Struthers can throw that pass with some pressure on him."

Lucky saw Malcolm grin. "Yeah, come and get me," he said. Though he sounded a little cocky, he was having fun, and all the guys seemed to like him.

The defense rushed hard. The running back pushed a shoulder into one rusher's chest and held him up long enough for Malcolm to get the pass off—a nice spiral. Philip made the catch look easy, and then pranced away. Lucky wished he could do that.

"Great job, Struthers," Coach Denton yelled. "You too, Romaine. That was a good block."

Lucky blocked an imaginary defender. The offense ran the play several times, and Lucky studied the way Romaine set his feet and used his arms. "Come on, defense," Johnny yelled. "Put some real pressure on him."

The defense made a better charge this time. Two of the biggest defensive linemen, Jerome and Carl, got into the backfield. Malcolm had to scramble to his left before he threw the ball, and the pass was behind the receiver.

"That's it, defense," Johnny yelled.

"Romaine, you let Carl get by you that time," Coach Denton shouted at the same time. "Square up, and stay in front of him. Keep your feet moving." He turned around. "Okay, let's get some of you other boys in here." He called out several names, and then, "Lucky, you got the idea? You ready to try?"

Lucky sprinted forward. His stomach fluttered wildly, but he wanted to get in the action.

And he did.

When the center hiked the ball, he set himself. Carl, who seemed to tower above Lucky, broke through the line. Lucky put a shoulder right into his gut — or at least he tried to. Actually, Carl's forearm cracked Lucky across the head and then a knee caught his chest. He hit the ground and curled up, afraid of feet. Other things whizzed by besides feet — like strange lights in his head. It took a while before the world stopped spinning.

"Are you all right?"

Lucky pulled his arms away from his eyes, rolled onto his back, and looked up at Coach Denton. "Yeah," he gasped, but he wasn't eager to stand up just yet. His eyes were seeing more people than he thought were really there.

The coach gave him a hand and pulled him up. "You were standing straight up, Lucky. As small as you are, you've got to bend forward and get some leverage."

"Okay." Lucky tried to figure out which direction he was facing. Why did the trees seem to be rotating?

"You want to try it again?"

"Yeah. Sure."

But as the offense huddled up, Lucky continued to stand where he was, still bent over, and when the players called him over, he started off in the wrong direction.

"Lucky, you'd better sit down for a minute. I think you got your bell rung."

"I think he'd better take up another game," Malcolm said. "Like checkers."

The boys laughed, but Coach Denton said, "That's enough, Struthers. Lucky's a determined kid. I can see it in his eyes."

That was strange because Lucky was trying to see through those eyes, which weren't exactly working right. But he managed to wander into the huddle, then back out to the formation. "On two," he told himself. "On two. Bend forward this time."

And then big Carl came crashing through again. Lucky saw nothing but knees. He felt the first impact, saw the explosion of light in his head—and then all the light died. The next time Lucky knew anything was when he heard a far-off voice say, "He's dead. Boy, oh, boy, Carl, you killed him."

"No, I didn't," Carl mumbled. "He's breathing—I think." He sounded worried.

Lucky felt fine. He was floating in golden light, and heads were drifting past him—lots of eyes, all looking very concerned.

"Do you know where you are?" the coach was saying. "Lucky, can you see me?"

"Sure," Lucky said, distantly. "As soon as it stops."

"What?"

"The park." But Lucky had found a point of focus. He could see Malcolm, looking maybe a little worried.

"He's too little," Malcolm said. "He's going to get killed."

"No, I'm fine," Lucky said. "Is Carl okay?"

The coach laughed first, and then everyone else. Lucky heard it all and wondered what was so funny. He planned to get up very soon now. He would just wait until he stopped floating. "I'm lucky," he said, mostly to himself. "I could have been hurt. But I don't feel a thing."

Then he heard Malcolm mutter to one of his friends, "I think the dude is brain dead. That's why."

Most everything was fuzzy in Lucky's mind, yet one thing was clear: making friends with this guy was not going to be easy.

CHAPTER 2

Ron Ladd was excited that his son, Lucky, was playing football. Of course, Lucky left out a few details about his blocks, and he forgot to mention that he hurt all over. The next morning, when a few things (like sitting, moving, and breathing) caused wild, shooting pains, he neglected to mention those too. *I'll be okay,* he thought. *In a few days, I'll be able to raise my arm high enough to brush my hair.* He could get a spoon to his mouth, however, so he did eat breakfast. "Dad, one thing," he said. "I need a mouthpiece. The coach said I could push my braces right through my lip."

"I thought this was flag football."

"It is. But those guys block pretty hard."

"Okay. I'll find a mouthpiece for you today." Lucky's dad took a huge chomp from a slice of toast and then talked with his mouth full. "I think you're going to be a star—just like I was."

"What did you play, Dad?"

"Left back."

"What's that?"

"That's what they did to me in school every year. Left me back with the same grade." He let out a thunderclap of a laugh that rattled the windows in the RV.

"That's a stupid joke, Dad," Lucky said, chuckling despite the pain.

"Then how come you're laughing?"

"Because I'm warped. I think you made me that way."

"Well, I've done my best." Dad must have liked that one too, because he cracked out another of his big laughs. Once he stopped laughing, he said, "I'll try to get to the game Saturday."

"You don't need to. I'm sure I won't play."

That was Lucky's hope. He figured with two days to rest, a game to watch, and then three days until the next practice, he'd be okay. That's how things would have gone, too, except that on Saturday the Pascal Pirates—his team—demolished the Alligators, a team from the tiny town of Atterbury, and the coach decided everyone should get a chance to play.

"Come here, Ladd," Coach Denton yelled. Lucky was standing well down the line. He pretended for a moment that he didn't hear. He was only just getting so he could turn his head anyway.

Dad said though, "Lucky, it's your coach. He wants you."

So Lucky ran—which reminded him how much his knees were hurting—down the sideline to the coach.

"Okay, watch the running back," Coach Denton said. "When you go in, do the same thing. You don't have to carry the ball. You just lead the blocking."

Lead the blocking? Lucky's stomach did a roll. He half-watched as the offense charged up to the line of scrimmage, afraid to see what the dangers might be.

"Are you going in?"

Lucky felt a nudge on his shoulder—and a pain shoot down his arm. Carl was grinning at him, his cheeks rounding into lumps. "Yeah, I guess so."

Lucky looked back to the game in time to see the ball hiked to Jud—the second-team quarterback. Malcolm was out of the game. Jud swept around the right end. Romaine led the way. When the defensive end rushed, Romaine put a shoulder into him, held him off long enough for Jud to get outside for a solid gain.

"See that, Lucky?" Coach Denton said. "Get in that end's way. Don't try to knock him down or anything. Just get between him and the ball carrier long enough to spring Jud outside."

"Okay." Lucky hopped up and down. He wasn't thinking about his pains now—except for the new ones he was discovering from hopping. "Should I go in?"

"Not yet. We'll come back to it. If we don't score before then."

So there was still hope. Maybe he wouldn't have to go in. All the same, he was so excited he bounced all over the place. He looked over to Dad, who gave him a big thumbs up.

"You'll do okay, Lucky," Carl said. "That guy's big, but he's slow. Just fall down in front of him and he'll trip."

"Oh, yeah, great plan, Carl."

Stick came up behind Lucky. "Be tough, my man," he said. "Put your head in his gut." All the boys laughed. Lucky looked around for Malcolm, who was standing with Winslow. He looked bored now that he knew he wouldn't play anymore.

"Hey, Lucky, don't hurt that guy," Philip said.

Lucky bounced on his toes. "Forget it. I'm going to punish him. The guy is dead meat." This went over big, and yet, Lucky knew he was just giving them more reasons to laugh at him.

The offense ran a pass that fell incomplete.

The coach walked closer to Lucky. "We'd better do it now. Tell Jud, 'Roll Eighteen.' That's the same play, only it goes the other way. Go in for Romaine."

Lucky was halfway to the huddle before the words sank in. What did "the other way" mean? How many ways were there? All he could do now was do what Romaine had done and hope for the best.

"Romaine, out," he yelled, the way he had heard the other guys do, and he jumped into the huddle. "Roll Eighteen," he said. "The other way."

"What? Roll Eighteen?"

"Yeah."

"Okay, let's break this one," Jud told the guys. "Roll Eighteen, on one." All the guys slapped their hands together, barked "Yo," then spun and charged to the line.

"Ready. Down. Hut, hut." The center hiked the ball, and Lucky cut to his right, running as hard as he could go. The end wasn't coming up this time. This would be easy. Suddenly, Lucky realized he was all alone. Everyone was running the opposite direction. He spun around and saw Jud—way out on the left side—being chased down behind the line of scrimmage.

Lucky didn't understand what had happened. Hadn't Jud gone the wrong way? Now another running back was sprinting toward him, yelling, "Ladd, out." Lucky ran off the field. As he approached the sideline, he saw that the guys were laughing. They slapped each other, making wise cracks; even the coach had a big grin.

"I said the other way," Coach Denton told Lucky.

"I wasn't sure what you meant by that. Which other way?"

"Left. We went right last time."

"Oh." Lucky didn't think his mistake was quite that funny. Guys didn't have to fall down on the ground. A person could laugh standing up. He turned around and faced the field, trying to ignore all the comments. He especially didn't want to look at Dad.

Then Lucky heard a voice and knew it was Malcolm's. "Maybe if we tie a pretty pink ribbon on his right hand, he'll be able to remember his left from his right."

Lucky took one long breath, and then he looked back at Malcolm. "Sorry I messed up," he said.

Most of the guys sensed that enough was

enough. They quieted down. Carl even said, "No
big deal, Lucky. We're way ahead."

But Malcolm said, "Hey, you're lucky. You
couldn't have blocked the guy anyway. At least you
saved yourself some pain."

"Hey, that's enough," Coach Denton said to
Malcolm. "That was my fault. Lucky needs to work
out with us a little more until he knows the plays.
I shouldn't have put him in."

Malcolm spoke softly, so that only the guys close
by could hear. "You shouldn't ever put him in. Unless you want him to bite someone. The only thing
big about him is his front teeth."

"Yeah," Winslow said. "They're all wired up for
strength." Some of the guys laughed.

Lucky thought maybe he had made a mistake.
Maybe Malcolm wasn't worth bothering with. There
had to be someone better in town he could make
friends with.

The next day, Lucky and his dad drove the RV
into Lafayette and went to church. The branch was
small but bigger than they had expected. People
came from a lot of small towns, as well as from the
city. Most of the talk was about the tornado. It had
cut an angling path west and north of the city, had
hit several little towns and some farms, and had
done a lot of damage to a mobile home park just

on the edge of Lafayette. Only three of the families in the branch had been hit, but two had lost their homes completely. Brother Giles, the branch president, spoke for several minutes at the beginning of sacrament meeting about the tremendous work the members had done in helping those who had sustained damage.

"I suppose it's what I expected," he said, "yet it was gratifying to see it. Almost all of you were out there within the next few days. Both the Hugos and the Stuvers said they had never felt so much love in their lives. The only thing is, we can't let up now. They still need plenty of our help." He explained some of the assignments for the coming week and said that the priesthood quorums and the Relief Society would be getting in touch with people. President Giles also introduced Brother Ladd and Lucky. He explained what they were doing in the area.

After the meeting, he came over to talk to them. "I guess you see a lot of this," he said.

"Well, yes, we do. Lucky and I have gotten so we see the bright side of these things. People show you what they're made of—and most of them are made of good stuff."

Brother Giles nodded. "Well, I sure was pleased. We've got a strange sort of combination in the branch—quite a few native Louisiana folks, some of 'em Cajuns, but then we've got our share of Northerners like me. Most of the local people are converts, and most of the rest aren't. It's the kind of combination that could make for a lot of division—and I guess sometimes we get some of that—but I surely didn't see any this week."

"Well, that's good to hear." The Struthers were coming into the foyer from the chapel. "We met the Struthers boy. He's playing football with Lucky. Are they the only black family?"

The branch president nodded toward the Struthers and gave them a little wave. He whispered, "Yes, they are. Lucky, you sure could help us there. Malcolm hasn't been happy here at all. I think he's needed someone his own age—a friend. Most of us have never been around . . . you know . . . blacks that much. I never know quite what to say to them."

"Say to them?" Dad said. "What do you mean?"

"Well, I guess I feel a little uncomfortable. They're well educated and all that. They're nice people. Don't get me wrong. I'm not prejudiced. I just . . . don't know how to talk to them."

"Malcolm told me he's not really a Mormon," Lucky said.

"Well, I think that's how he probably thinks of it. But he's a member. He's been baptized."

Lucky looked at the Struthers. Malcolm's father was tall and well dressed, and his mother was beautiful. She wore an expensive-looking pale yellow dress. Both seemed almost too young to have a child Malcolm's age. A girl two or three years younger than Malcolm stood half-hiding just behind Sister Struthers. Malcolm didn't look at Lucky. He walked to the front doors.

"Lucky's the best guy in the world to help with something like that," Brother Ladd said. "Let's go talk to them."

Dad patted Brother Giles on the shoulder, and then he took about four of his giant steps across the foyer. "Hello, Brother Struthers. I saw your son play on Saturday. I just wanted to meet you and your wife."

Brother Struthers extended his hand and nodded. "Nice to know you," he said softly. Sister Struthers reached out her hand too, smiled, and said, "Happy to meet you." Lucky thought they seemed a little shy—not at all like Malcolm.

"Lucky's playing football too. The boys seem to have a fine team. I really like the coach."

"Yes, the coach is a very nice man." Brother Struthers sounded Northern. He also appeared hesitant, or maybe just quiet by nature. "Well, very nice to meet you," he said. "I hope you have a good stay here."

"Yes. Maybe I'll see you at the ball games."

"Yes. I'll be there sometimes."

"Nice to meet you," Sister Struthers said and smiled again. She and her husband walked away.

Lucky looked up at his dad. "See what I mean?" he said.

"No. What?"

"They didn't want to talk to us. They're just like Malcolm."

"Oh, I think they . . . well, I'm not sure. Maybe it wasn't that. Maybe they just don't blab a lot the way you and I do."

"It seemed as if they were nervous, or something."

"Well, sure. It's not every day people meet important guys like you and me." He gave Lucky a little knock on the shoulder.

Lucky really wished he hadn't done that. The ache in his shoulders was surpassed only by the soreness in the rest of his body. "Dad, I'm serious. I told you that I tried to make friends with Malcolm, and all he's done is treat me like he can't stand me."

"I know. But now you have to give it another shot. Brother Giles just asked you to."

Lucky had to admit that was true. And he still wanted to think that it was something he could do. Still, he also wanted to learn to play football, and right now his chances for success looked about the same for either project.

CHAPTER 3

"**D**ad?"

"Yeah."

Lucky and his dad had polished off their traditional Sunday Shake 'n' Bake chicken dinner, with nothing-but-lettuce salad, and Dad was reading the newspaper. Lucky lay on his bed, trying to read a book, but he was thinking more about Malcolm.

"I think Malcolm doesn't like me because I'm white."

"Oh, I doubt that. What makes you think so?"

"He said he didn't need any white friends."

"Is that right?" Dad put down his paper. He was sitting at the kitchen table, which actually jutted into the living room area. Light shone through the window, right through Dad's hair—which wasn't quite so full as it once was. "It sounds as if Malcolm is struggling right now to know where he fits in.

Maybe that's why he doesn't feel comfortable with the Church—since all the members of the branch are white."

"So what am I supposed to do? I've been thinking about it, and I don't think he'll ever be friends with me."

"It sounds to me like you've lucked out again."

"Hey, don't even say it. I know the whole speech: This is a challenge, and challenges are great because I can learn lots of stuff. By now, I ought to be a genius, according to your theory."

"So, don't you believe it?"

"I'd rather get a little of the kind of luck where I don't have to learn so much."

"Naw, you don't mean that. That's a wimp's kind of luck." He grinned.

"Maybe I'm really a wimp, then."

"No way. You're the crash-land-get-up-and-go-again kid."

"I don't want to crash land. I want to do something right for a change."

"Lucky, my boy," and now Dad looked a little more serious, "you do lots of things right. You're smart, you're—"

"You said I'm average. You even said that was the best way to be."

"Well, you're way above average for an average kid. That's the best combination I know of."

"Except that it doesn't make any sense."

"It does to me, and I'm a pretty smart guy myself, so it must make sense." He laughed again, loud enough to set off vibrations. Then he added seriously, "Lucky, the only thing you can do is show Malcolm what a good friend is like. I think he'll respond to that."

"Yeah? Maybe."

At school on Monday, most of the guys were friendly when they teased, but they still teased. When recess came, a lot of the boys headed out to play touch football. Lucky needed to give his body a rest, so he wandered off to see what other kids were doing. Most of them were in groups, playing or talking.

As he walked by the monkey bars, he saw a girl, also by herself. She was sitting on a cross bar, staring out across the playground, or maybe just lost in her thoughts. She was not someone Lucky had seen before.

"Hi," Lucky said.

The girl glanced over, ever so briefly. "Hi," she said, or maybe, "Hey." But she didn't smile, didn't even pay any real attention. She wasn't the sort of girl who would grow up to be a movie star. She was just sort of regular: limp brown hair, pale green eyes, and faded clothes.

"Are you okay?"

"What?"

"You look sad. I just wondered if you were okay."

The girl looked surprised. "Who are you?" she said. She had about as strong an accent as Lucky had heard, but not Cajun.

"My name's Lucky Ladd. I just moved here."

"What grade you in?"

"Sixth."

"No, you ain't," she said.

"Yeah. I am."

She nodded. "I guess you wouldn't lie about it."

"Are you sad?" Lucky asked again.

"Why?"

"You look sad."

"I never heard a boy ask a girl somethin' like that before. Or 'nother boy neither."

"Really?"

"Where you from?" she asked.

"Well, I used to live in Utah. That's where I grew up, and it's nice out there. But my dad moves all the time now, so I end up in a different place every month or two."

"That's weird."

"Yeah. I guess it is, sort of. Sometimes I wish we could just stay in one place longer, but Dad says we're lucky because we get to see so many places, and I know I'm lucky because that's my name."

It was his old joke, but maybe he hadn't said it quite right because she just stared at him. Finally she said, "You're weird. You know that?"

Lucky grinned and then realized he was flashing enough metal to build a skyscraper. Still, he said, "Well, you're not the first person to tell me that." He shrugged. "I guess you're right, though. There's not too much normal about me. Except I'm about average. Not too smart; not too dumb."

"You sound perty smart to me. How come you came here?"

"Because of the tornado. My dad works for an insurance company."

"He's prob'ly comin' to our house then. Our house got blowed away."

"Really?" Lucky said again. He walked a little closer and leaned against the bars. The girl had her head down, her chin resting on the back of her hand, which lay lightly on a crossbar. "Did you lose everything?"

"Jist 'bout. We found some stuff. But mos' ever'thin' was all ruined from the rain 'n' hail."

"You must live west of town—where the worst damage was."

"Yup. We got a little farm, jist on the edge of town."

"Was anyone hurt?"

"Nope. We was in the cellar. Then we come up 'n' the whole roof was gone. Most of the walls too."

Lucky had heard that kind of story hundreds of times. He didn't know why it sounded sadder this time. "No wonder you're feeling down," he said. "I'm sure I would too. But those things work out all right."

The girl raised her head. "You're the weirdest boy I ever met," she said, but she smiled just a little. Her face looked so much brighter when she smiled, and her green eyes weren't quite so pale.

"Why?"

"I jist never heard a boy say nothin' like that before."

"Oh." Lucky was used to the idea that he didn't do things quite the way most guys his age did. Dad said it was from being around him—a grownup—too much. Yet he never thought of himself as that different. "I just . . . well, I see lots of people go through stuff like this. Usually it turns out okay. I knew this one boy who lost his goldfish in a flood. And I said, 'The fish are probably happier now anyway—not being in a bowl.' He said they'd never make it without him feeding them every day, but I said they probably would."

She was staring again. "Where'd you come here from—I mean, the last place?"

"California."

"Really? Did you like it there?"

"Yeah."

"Better'n here?"

"Uh . . . yeah. I guess I did."

"What's wrong with Pascal?" She smiled a little more now. She had dimples, it turned out.

"Nothing." Lucky didn't want to tell the whole story, but he was in a bit deep. "Some of the guys around here don't seem to like me."

"How come?"

Lucky laughed. "You say I ask questions, but you're the one doing all of that."

Now she laughed. "I ask reg'lar questions. You ask weird ones. How come the boys don't like you?"

"I don't know. Because I'm small, I guess, and I'm not a very good football player. I'm getting better, but—"

"That's how the boys are. If you was some great big guy, 'n' you could help 'em win football games, they'd think you was the best thing that ever hit town. That's the on'y thing they care 'bout—foot-ball."

Lucky nodded. He thought that might be true.

"I don't have any friends, and I've lived here all my life."

"Why not?"

She wasn't ready to answer, or wasn't willing. She hunched her shoulders, and Lucky saw the look return—the sadness in her eyes.

"I'll be your friend."

"Oh, brother. You are weird."

"What's weird about that?" Lucky saw he had embarrassed her—she wouldn't look at him.

"Girls aren't friends with boys—not in sixth grade anyhow."

"Hey, I had a good friend in California. Tiffany. She's a girl. She's in sixth grade."

"Maybe out there. Not here."

"I didn't mean we had to hang around together all the time or anything. I just meant—you know—we could . . . be friends."

"You mean like girlfriend and boyfriend?" Her face, even her neck, were suddenly glowing red.

"Oh, no. I didn't mean that."

She laughed hard this time.

"What's so funny?"

"Nothin'." But she kept laughing. Then she slid

slowly off the bar she was on, crouched to get under another bar, and stepped out toward Lucky. When she straightened up, Lucky thought he knew why she had been laughing. She was tall—almost as tall as Malcolm and some of the bigger guys. Lucky didn't even come up to her shoulders.

"Wow," Lucky said.

"What's that s'pposed to mean?"

"You're taller than I thought."

"Is that bad?" She was still blushing.

"It's just . . . how it is."

"Well, you may be taller someday, but I'm not gettin' any shorter. So I guess you're the lucky one, jist like your name."

"What's so bad about being tall?"

"The boys been callin' me "Beanpole" 'n' stuff like that since I was in first grade."

"That's stupid. They all want to be tall. I'd give anything in this entire world if I could grow one foot, very fast."

"Sure, but if a girl's tall, boys think it's funny."

"Or if a guy's short."

"Right." And there they stood. She put her hands on her hips and looked down at him. "If we could jist switch, ever'thing would be all right."

"If we weren't us, we'd miss ourselves after a while."

"What?"

Lucky let it go. "What's your name?" he asked.

"Sharon Talbot."

"Okay, Sharon. We're friends."

"Don't tell anybody you said that to me."

"Why?"

"Jist don't."

"But are we friends or aren't we?"

"I don't know. It's too weird, if you ask me." She walked away.

Lucky pushed his hands into his pockets, just stood there for a moment, and thought what he had planned to do. He turned to check on what the guys were doing now, and he saw some of them coming across the playground. Malcolm was leading the group, but Winslow was the one who said, "Hey, Lucky, I see you found yourself a girl."

Lucky didn't say anything.

"You could climb up on a ladder and give her a big smooch."

Lucky didn't want to let these guys think they were getting to him. "I think I'll wait until I get my braces off," he said. "I wouldn't want to hurt anyone with all these wires."

Most of the guys laughed—even Winslow. But Malcolm didn't. He said, "What were you and Beanpole talking about?"

"Her name's Sharon," Lucky said.

"She's the stupidest girl in this school."

"Hey, come on," Lucky said. "That's not—"

"It's true," Malcolm said. "She's a stupid country girl."

"You know, Malcolm, you . . . "

"I what?"

Lucky decided not to say it. He remembered what he had promised Brother Giles—and his dad. He watched Malcolm's eyes—the bullets. Lucky always had the feeling Malcolm was trying to see just how far he could push him.

"I what? What were you going to say?"

Lucky shrugged. "Nothing."

"Good answer," Winslow said. "You say anything else and Malcolm'll knock your head off."

All the guys laughed, and then Stick reached down and patted Lucky on the shoulder. "You're short enough without losing your head," he said.

"Hey, no way," Malcolm said. "I'd be a real jerk if I beat up on a kid the size of my little sister."

Lucky thought of saying, "You are a jerk, Malcolm. You don't need me to help you." But he didn't. He just turned and walked away.

CHAPTER 4

On Tuesday, after school, the team practiced again. Lucky had gotten so he could move without hurting, and he sure didn't need to get pounded once more, but he wasn't about to quit. So Lucky wore his sweats to school, with shorts underneath, and took his mouthpiece. The only trouble was that, when he put it in, he could hardly keep his mouth shut. His teeth stuck out in front anyway, but with a layer of wire and another of plastic, he looked as if he had a baseball in his mouth.

A lot of the players seemed to like Lucky, but no one took him seriously. Big Carl got to the park early, and he was quick to give Lucky a slam in the back and assure him that everything would go better today. He was the only one who didn't tease him.

Philip also got there early. "Hey, Lucky," he

said. "How ya' doing today?" He was chuckling, as though the question were some sort of put-down.

"I'm okay."

"So what's with Malcolm? What's he got against you?"

"I don't know. He seems to think I'm small and can't play very well. I don't know where he got that idea."

Philip laughed. "You're all right, Lucky," he said. "Don't let Malcolm git ya' down."

"Don't worry. I won't." Actually, what he told himself was that he was going to prove to Malcolm that he could play the game. That would be the beginning of getting his respect.

During scrimmage, Lucky watched everything, listened to every word. He went through the motions on the sidelines, imitating Romaine's moves. The other boys on the sidelines were mostly small too, or clumsy, and they thought Lucky was great entertainment. A kid named Bobby Joe, or Billy Bob, or one of those kinds of names, kept telling Lucky, "That's it, you practice over here. It's a lot safer."

Mainly Lucky tried to ignore them. He was waiting for his chance.

And it came.

"Okay, Lucky," Coach Denton called out, "do

you want to come in now and try some of these plays?"

Lucky trotted over to the coach, where the offense was huddling up. One of the boys on defense, a Cajun kid named Robert, shouted, "Hey, Lucky, what's that thing you got in your mouth—a watermelon?"

Jerome, one of Robert's buddies, yelled, "Hey, Lucky, you'd better make out your will. Leave your sweats to me. My little brother can wear 'em."

"All right, you guys," the coach barked, "that's enough!" He stepped around the huddle and pointed his finger. "I'm not going to have any of that stuff. You hear me?"

When Lucky broke the huddle and ran to his position, he was ready and determined. He gritted his teeth—or at least he bit down hard on the plastic—and squinted. He doubled his fists against his knees, tried to find some rage within himself. "All right, someone's going to pay," he told himself. "I'm putting one of those guys on his back."

The play was a sweep to the left—the play he'd messed up in the game. Lucky understood now what he had to do. He watched Malcolm take the hike, then broke to the left to lead the blocking. He saw Jerome come up and knew this was it. He was ready to plow him under when something hit his foot, and suddenly he was on his face. Lucky took a few seconds to realize that Malcolm had stepped on his heel and knocked him down.

"Hey, man, you got to move."

Lucky was busy pulling his face out of the grass. He was glad for the mouthpiece now.

"Come on, Malcolm, you did that on purpose," Lucky heard the coach say.

"No way. The kid's so slow, I couldn't stay behind him. He never would have made the block anyway."

"Malcolm, that's enough. You have to wait for a block sometimes. That's part of running with the ball."

As Lucky walked back to the huddle, Malcolm said, "Next time, move it, or I'll run up your back."

Lucky didn't respond.

"Okay, Malcolm," Coach Denton said. "Let's run I-29 and give Lucky a chance to carry the ball."

"Good idea," he said and glanced at Winslow. Lucky saw him smile, just a little.

"Lucky, this is a pitch-out to you. It's almost the same play we ran last time, except the guard pulls and leads the blocking and you carry the ball. Let's take it around the right end. Your blockers will get out there and knock some guys down. I think guys are going to have trouble getting hold of your flags. You'll be our secret weapon."

The coach was teasing a little, but Lucky liked having his chance. He could show something now. Maybe blocking was hard for him, yet if he could dodge around enough, he could keep his flags and go for a long run.

Lucky remembered what Romaine had done when they ran the play earlier. He started to the right and watched for the pitch. It came a little hard, however, and in front of him. Lucky reached out and tipped the ball high in the air. He was able to run under it and catch it—almost. Just as he was about to take off with the football, the thing somehow slithered through his arms, down his body, and onto the grass. He stopped, picked it up, dropped it, picked it up again, and then looked up to see two tacklers coming hard from the right side. He sprinted to the left, reversing the play.

The defense had been pulled to the right, and suddenly Lucky was in the open, moving around the left. His feet, though, seemed stuck to the ground— or the other guys were flying—because they soon closed off his path. He was running straight toward three defenders, and no blocker was in sight. Suddenly Lucky threw on his brakes, stopped dead, and reversed again, heading right. But guys were over there too.

Lucky was surrounded, so he simply turned the play upfield and waited for the worst. Then something wonderful happened. A hole opened up straight down the center of the field. Lucky charged forward, reached the line of scrimmage, then broke loose into the clear. It was touchdown time — he had finally done something right. He began to think about spiking the ball. This was one of the great moments, one of the great thrills of his life. He was running, leaving everyone behind, charging straight toward the goal line . . . until he tripped and fell down.

More tragic things had happened in the history of the world, but at the moment, Lucky couldn't see how anything could be worse. He pulled himself up from the ground and got ready to take the abuse. Everyone, however, was laughing too hard to say anything. Jerome was down on his hands and knees. Robert was draped over him, limp as a dummy, except that he shook all over. Then Lucky saw the coach. He was bent over, his hands on his knees, laughing so hard that the bald spot on the top of his head had turned bright red.

So I fell down? Is it really that funny? So I had my big chance and tripped? Is that the joke of the century? I've seen NFL running backs fall down. It happens. Don't these guys watch games on television?

Lucky walked back to where the huddle was supposed to be. He pulled his mouthpiece out. "Sorry," he said to Coach Denton.

"Hey, Lucky, I'm sorry to laugh. It was just— you know—after all that running around, and then finally getting in the open, and . . . well, you know."

Not far away, Lucky heard Malcolm's voice, "He may be little, and he may be slow, but at least he's clumsy."

Lucky managed a bit of a smile, even though he didn't really want to. "No one got my flag," he said.

That night, at dinner, Lucky told his dad that practice had gone fine. He didn't have the heart to tell him what had really happened. He did say, finally, "Dad, I don't think I'll ever be friends with Malcom. I don't even think I like him."

"Well, he's been pretty tough on you. But I think you need to try to figure out why. There may be a lot more to it than you understand right now."

"Maybe he's just a jerk."

Dad laughed. "Well, just give him some time. He may come around yet."

"Yeah, he'll probably call up tonight to see if I want to come over to watch the Disney Channel."

Dad burst into one of his thirteen-on-the-Richter-scale laughs. "Yeah, he might. Or maybe you ought to call him up to see if he wants to play some Go Fish with you. Or maybe some Old Maid."

"I think he'd rather invent a new game called Go Jump in a Lake," Lucky said, but he was smiling now. Dad always knew how to make him do that.

Lucky did his homework after supper. When he was finished, he wrote postcards to his friends Tiffany and Calvin in Shoreside, California—the last town he had lived in. "I miss you," he told them, and it wasn't just something a guy writes on a card.

Dad, though, saw what he was doing and said, "Hey, are you writing to your girl?"

"Dad, Tiffany is not my girl. We're just—"

"Don't give me that. You should hear what you say about her in your sleep."

Lucky was stunned for a moment. Maybe he really did . . . naw, Dad was putting him on. "What did I say?"

"You said, 'Tiffany, take my heart.'" He extended his hands as though he were handing over something.

"I did not."

"That's what it sounded like."

"No way."

"Well, I don't know. Maybe you said, 'Timpani, hate my tark.' It was something like that."

"What're you talking about? What's a 'tark'?"

"Don't ask me. You said it."

Oh, brother. Lucky tried not to laugh—but he couldn't help it.

Things didn't get any better at the practice Thursday. In fact, Malcolm and some of the other teammates kept up the teasing until Coach Denton stopped practice and made everyone gather around him. "Let me tell you guys somethin'," he said. "No one on this team works harder than Lucky. He does everything I tell him, and he learns real fast. I saw his dad at the game last Saturday. He's a great big guy. Chances are Lucky'll be as big as anyone here. When that happens, he'll be a heckuva player, because he's learning his technique at a time when he has to use every ounce of strength he's got."

Lucky could have lived without this. He knew what the guys were thinking, even if they were keeping their mouths shut.

"And Malcolm," the coach said. He took a step closer to him. "You've got enough ability to be great, if that's what you want. But you'd rather put some guy down with your mouth than put him down fair and square on the field. I don't know why a guy with your talent wants to be like that."

Malcolm looked at his feet. Lucky felt that the coach had finally gotten to him. Still, when practice was over, there was the voice again—the same tone. "Hey, Lucky, it must be nice to be the coach's little pet." And there was the same laughter, not just from Malcolm, but from his friends.

"I saw you talking to Sharon again today," Winslow said. "I think you got something going with her. If you grow up big and tall, like the coach says you will, maybe you can marry her."

Lucky kept walking.

"Isn't that what you're hoping for, little Lucky? Don't you want to marry Beanpole?"

Lucky still didn't say anything. He kept going.

Then he heard Malcolm. "Lucky's a good Mormon. He loves everybody. That's why he won't fight back."

Lucky turned around. "Maybe I'm a Mormon like some of those guys in the Book of Mormon— who could take on a whole army and slay 'em all."

Everyone laughed, even Malcolm. "Go ahead and try," he said.

"Not right now. I'm not in a slaying mood." He turned around and walked away.

"You keep it up, little guy," Malcolm said, "and you'd better be in a running mood." He didn't sound angry, though. He seemed to get a kick from Lucky standing up to him for a moment.

CHAPTER 5

Lucky and his dad ate out that night. They didn't do that very often, but Dad was late getting home, and he said he really didn't feel like cooking. So they went to a little restaurant—not fast food; there really weren't any fast-food places in Pascal. The restaurant was a large diner specializing in seafood and Cajun cooking.

The waiter who came to the table was a husky man in a half-unbuttoned white shirt. His chest was covered with thick, curly hair. The first time he spoke, Lucky didn't understand a word, and his Dad said, "Excuse me?"

"Hello. How you feeling tonight?"

"Oh. Fine."

"That's good. What I get for you?"

Dad said he wanted to try some Cajun cooking,

and the man said he might like the blackened red fish or some kind of crawfish.

"What's black and red fish?" Lucky asked.

"No, Lucky," his dad said. "It's blackened. It's the way they cook it—in pepper and spices."

The waiter laughed. "That's right. It's good stuff. You like it."

"What's the Crawfish A-too something?"

"Eh-too-feh—étouffée. That's very good too. You get rice, and the crawfish is cooked in nice sauce. I think you like that best."

So Lucky said he'd give the crawfish a try, even though he was a little worried about eating one. He had rolled a few rocks off what he had called "crawdaddies" back in Utah. He had always chased them or used them for fish bait when he caught any. They hadn't looked like anything he wanted to eat.

When the waiter left, Lucky said, "Dad, how long do you think we'll be in Pascal?"

"It's hard to say. The damage isn't really too widespread, and most of the places that were hit were wiped out entirely. It doesn't take long to appraise those. But there were cars with some damage, and a few houses that didn't get hit directly."

"Did you look at a farmhouse, just outside of town? The family is named Talbot."

"Yes. I've got the coverage on that place. Did you meet the son or something?"

"The daughter."

"What's this? My son has already met another woman? What's Tiffany going to say?"

"No, it wasn't like that."

"That's what you said about Tiffany, but I saw that glow in your eyes."

"No, really. Just tell me. How bad is her place?"

"Well, there wasn't much left. But then, there wasn't much to start with. Those poor people were living in nothing more than a shack. And they've got five or six kids."

"Maybe they're sort of lucky. Maybe they'll have a better house now." Lucky really wanted to believe that.

"Yeah. The only trouble is, they didn't have much coverage. They may not get enough to build anything—unless they can do their own work."

Lucky shook his head. "Sometimes things don't seem fair, Dad. Storms come through, and it's as if they pick some people to mess up and leave the next ones just fine. Then some other guy, who builds houses for a living—or something like that—he comes out great."

"I know." Lucky expected one of Dad's little speeches about good things coming out of bad experiences, but instead he said, "I'll check on the Talbot place. Sometimes a builder will help out— or maybe Church members around here could do something."

"That'd be great." Lucky felt good about that, and he felt good about his dad, who always tried to help when he could. "I saw in the paper that two people got killed," he said.

"Yeah. They were in a mobile home park that got torn up. One of them was just a little baby."

"Don't you get tired of seeing stuff like that?"

Dad had just taken a big gulp of water. He bumped the glass back down on the table. "Sure I do. I walk into places where a family has lost everything. I see people searching through rubble trying to find the family picture album or some picture off the wall. Yet when you talk to them, the first thing they say is, 'But we're alive, and we still have each other.' All the stuff people keep trying to get hold of gets blown away, and then for the first time, they see what they really care about."

"What about when people get killed?"

"Well, that's harder, but it's not exactly different. People go through some real agony when they lose their loved ones, but they take another, different look at things. They think about what life means. And they usually find they have more strength than they thought they had."

"When Mom died, I didn't feel strong. I just felt like I wanted to cry forever, and never do one more thing."

"But what did you do?"

Lucky shrugged. "Well, I didn't cry forever."

"And you're a tougher kid because of it."

"I know. Still, I sometimes just wish there were no tornados and no fires, and no babies getting killed, and . . . no cancer."

"No you don't, Lucky. When you think about it right, you understand why all those things happen in this world."

Lucky wasn't so sure. But he knew what his father would say.

"So how is football going?"

"Bad."

"What's so bad about it?"

"I don't know. I just keep messing up."

"Messing up? How?"

"I don't know. Like the other day, I had a chance to make a good run, but I tripped and fell on my face." Lucky had thought he wouldn't tell his dad about that, yet sooner or later he usually told him just about everything.

"You mean you were carrying the ball?"

"Yeah."

"Hey, that's great."

"What's so great about it? I messed up the play."

"Naw. You just tripped. That happens to everybody. I'm glad the coach is giving you a chance to
play. And you picked up some big yards before you
tripped, didn't you?"

"Yeah."

"Hey, well, that's good. You could've gotten
thrown for a loss, you know."

"If I had, you'd say that'd make a better player
out of me."

Dad laughed in a sudden burst, his voice ringing
around the room. People turned to look at him.
Lucky was used to that. "Yeah," he said. "I probably would. You're on to me, Lucky."

Lucky laughed in spite of himself. Dad nearly
always made him feel better—even when Lucky
wanted to feel sorry for himself. "I've been on to
you for a long time," he said.

"Yeah, I guess so. You're too smart for me.
God's given you plenty, you know. I hope you don't
forget that."

"Just average—remember?"

"Above average for an average kid—remember?"

Lucky shook his head, while his father chuckled,

and then he took a sip of his water and looked around. Not many people were in the restaurant, but in another room a band was playing, or perhaps warming up. One guy was playing a fiddle, really going after it. Lucky liked the feel of the place. The waiter was at another table now, talking and laughing, using his Cajun language. Lucky couldn't understand him, but he liked him. He wondered why people couldn't just be nice to each other all the time.

"Dad, the guys on the team are still giving me a bad time."

"You mean teasing or what?"

"Yeah, but it's not just that. Malcolm says something rotten to me every time he gets a chance."

"What does he say?"

"I don't remember exactly. He's been making fun of me because he saw me talking to Sharon Talbot. She's a lot taller than I am. He's been calling her names too."

Dad let his breath out slowly, leaned forward, and looked at Lucky closely. "I know guys are cruel sometimes. Especially in a group, when they start showing off. But I'll bet Malcolm's not so bad once you get to know him."

"I don't know about that, Dad."

"Really?"

"Well, he's not so bad around the other guys. I can see why maybe they like him."

"Lucky, you've really lucked out this time. I've got a feeling you're going to learn something important in little old Pascal."

Lucky didn't think so—unless he was learning something about himself he'd never even suspected before. "Do you think I'm prejudiced against Malcolm?"

"Are you talking about racial prejudice?"

"Yeah."

"You'd have to answer that yourself."

"I don't think I like any of the black guys on the team—except maybe Philip. So maybe I am prejudiced."

"Are any of the white guys on the team giving you a hard time?"

"Yeah."

"Do you hate all the white guys?"

"No." Lucky thought about that. "But Malcolm doesn't like me because I'm white. Maybe it's the same with those other black guys."

"So you think they are prejudiced?"

"Maybe."

"Well, Lucky, prejudice mean 'pre-judge.' I wouldn't make up your mind too fast. That's prejudging."

Lucky thought about that. "Well, I don't know," he finally said. "Maybe it has nothing to do with being white. Maybe they don't like guys who are short, slow, clumsy, and have tinsel teeth sticking out farther than their noses."

Dad let out another one of his room-shaking laughs, then said, "Or maybe they're jealous because they've never met such a terrific guy before."

"Yeah, right."

"I'll tell you how to solve this problem, okay?"

"Okay."

"What did you do when you fell off your skateboard in Shoreside?"

"I don't know."

"Come on. What did you do?"

"I just got up and—"

"That's exactly what you did. And that's what you always do—right?"

"I guess so."

"Okay. Those guys want to see what you're made of. That's how boys usually are." He sat quietly, looking at Lucky for a time. "Of course, I already know what you're made of."

"I know what I'm made of too. We learned about that in science. Mostly water and a few minerals and stuff."

Dad laughed again, shaking the table. Again

everyone looked at them. Lucky thought that some things never change.

In a few more minutes the food came. Lucky decided he liked crawfish. The étouffée was good stuff. He tried Dad's blackened red fish and liked that too. At least something in Louisiana was turning out right.

Lucky and his dad walked home slowly, enjoying the cool evening air and the pretty fall colors. Lucky felt comfortable. That was one good thing about Dad—Lucky almost always felt good when he was with him. When they had nearly reached the RV, Dad said he needed to make a phone call. He stopped at a booth, looked in the phone book for a number, and made the call. He talked quite some time, and when he came back out, he said, "Well, that should turn out to be interesting."

"What?"

"I just invited the Struthers over for one of my famous spaghetti dinners."

"They're coming to the RV for dinner?"

"Yup."

Lucky couldn't believe it. "Dad, why'd you do that?"

"It seemed like a good idea," he said, grinning.

"I just changed my mind."

"Changed your mind? About what?"

"You're not such a great father after all."

Dad shook a few more leaves off the surrounding trees with his laugh, and Lucky even laughed, though he didn't want to.

CHAPTER 6

*T*he Struthers came over on Friday evening. They were nice, but they still seemed a little nervous. Dad was wearing an old BYU sweatshirt and jeans. Brother Struthers had on an expensive-looking sweater, and Sister Struthers was wearing a knit dress and fancy, dangling ear rings. Even Malcolm had on his church slacks, and his little sister, who kept trying to hide behind Malcolm, had her hair done up in pig tails and red ribbons.

"So how are you doing?" Lucky's father boomed.

Brother Struthers spoke in a controlled sort of voice—like a radio announcer's. "We're just fine, thank you. How are you?"

"We're doing fine. We like this area. It's very interesting. How long did you say you've been down here?"

"Just over a year."

"Do you like it?"

"Well, it's different from what we're accustomed to."

"Sit down. Sit down." Dad motioned toward the sofa that was also Lucky's bed. "Relax for a minute. I've got my world famous, straight-out-of-a-bottle-but-add-some-stuff spaghetti sauce heating up. Lucky made the salad. I hope you don't like a lot of extras in your salad. We're straight lettuce guys."

Sister Struthers smiled and said that would be fine, and she laughed, softly. Dad, of course, was making the RV rock with his laugh. She sat down, and her little daughter, who was four or so, slid into the seat next to her.

"Did you see Lucky's bug collection, right over your heads there? Malcolm, you'll want to take a look at that."

Sister Struthers only glanced up, but Brother Struthers stood and took a careful look at the bottles. Malcolm had been about to sit down at the little built-in table behind the driver's seat, but he went over by his dad now.

"Well," Brother Struthers said, "that's quite a collection. I don't think I've seen some of these." He pointed to a bottle with an exotic-looking beetle inside.

"I got that in Florida," Lucky said. "Most of the people who live there said they'd never seen one either."

"Yes, I can imagine." He sat down and nodded to Lucky, as a sign of congratulations. Malcolm kept his back turned to Lucky, and he kept looking at the bottles. Dad was busy for the moment, stirring his sauce and checking on the boiling spaghetti.

When it came time to eat, there was barely room for all six to crowd around the little table. Dad joked about that. The Struthers said it was fine — and they were very nice — but they were almost too polite.

Malcolm said nothing. Dad asked him all about the football team, but he answered as briefly as he could. "It's just flag," he finally said. "I'm waiting to play real football." Dad gave up and started quizzing Brother Struthers about his work.

When everyone had finished eating, Dad said, "If you guys want to go out and throw a ball around, you might as well."

For a moment Malcolm didn't move from his seat, but Lucky got his football. He went to the door before he realized that Malcolm wasn't following. "Go ahead," his dad said, and Malcolm finally got up. But outside, he shut the door and then, as though he were finally free to take off his mask, gave Lucky a look of disgust—the one Lucky was used to.

"Don't you want to throw the ball around?"

Malcolm shrugged. "It doesn't matter."

Lucky stepped back a little and flipped the ball to him. He kept walking back as Malcolm gripped the ball and threw a little pass back to him.

Malcolm had to chase Lucky's pass, which hit the pavement and bounced past him. The sun was near setting, and the buildings and trees close by cast long shadows. The light was beginning to fail, so the boys didn't ever get too far apart. Or maybe it was because Lucky had trouble gripping a football and couldn't throw very far. For a time they just stood facing each other, throwing back and forth. Malcolm made the toss seem easy, but Lucky had to work to throw the ball every time.

"I can't throw a good spiral," Lucky said. "My hand is too small."

Malcolm nodded, then put something extra on his throw, maybe to show off his own spiral. Something about that kind of cockiness really bothered Lucky. "Look, I know you didn't want to come over here. You don't have to do this if you don't want to." He tossed the ball. Malcolm caught it, held it, and glared at Lucky.

For a time the two boys just looked at each

other. The cicadas had begun to set up their evening chant, and flying insects circled through the moist, yellow light. Malcolm was silhouetted against the reflection on the silver side of the RV.

"I know you don't like me, Malcolm," Lucky said. "But if you don't like me because I'm white, you're prejudiced."

Malcolm smiled, just slightly. "Yeah, right. You just love me, don't you? I'm your brother, no matter what color I am."

Lucky walked forward, with his hands tucked in his back pockets. "I guess you're saying that you think I'm prejudiced against you."

"I'll tell you what I'm saying. Don't try to act like we're friends—'cause we're not."

"I don't get that. I don't see why we can't be."

Malcolm tossed the football into the air, just a foot or so, catching it in the other hand. "Lucky, you act like you don't know how things are—but you know. Everybody knows."

"I don't know what you're talking about."

Malcolm took another step closer, and Lucky saw the rage as he bit his words off, one at a time. "White people act like they can be friends with us. But they don't mean it. Not deep down."

"That's not true, Malcolm. I've met lots of—"

"Don't tell me, Lucky. I know what I'm talking

about. Things are divided up. That's how it was in Chicago, and that's how it is here."

Lucky thought about that. "Maybe to some degree, Malcolm. But look how the guys treat you at school. You're the big shot. Everybody—"

"I'm good at football, that's all. But I got to stick with the black guys if I'm going to have any real friends. When I first got down here, everybody was on my back. They didn't like my clothes, the way I talked—nothing. I had to find somebody who didn't care about all that."

"Yeah, right. Then I come in, and you dump on me the same way."

"No. You came in asking who the Mormons were. That's a white church, Lucky. My friends all know that."

"No, it isn't. There's every race in our church."

"Yeah, right."

Lucky didn't know what to say. He'd never thought about the things Malcolm was saying. "Aren't people nice to you at church?" he asked.

Malcolm laughed. "You don't get it, Lucky. You never will."

"Do the people at church—"

"Lucky, listen to me. Here's how it is. I'm going to your church as long as my parents make me—then never again. I know who my real friends are—

and they're not all those white people who grin at me at the Mormon church. I know how they act, but I know what they really think of me."

"But it seems to me if you—"

"Lucky, I've said all I'm going to say. I won't give you a bad time at practice anymore—and I won't at school. But don't try to hang around me."

Lucky gave up. He didn't know why that bothered him so much, but he did decide to quit trying.

So they threw the football until it was too dark, and when they finally went inside, they found that Malcolm's parents were standing at the door, ready to leave. Brother Struthers was holding his little daughter in his arms, and he was speaking quietly, thanking Brother Ladd.

Something had changed. Lucky heard it in the voices. Sister Struthers said, "This has meant a lot to us. I wish you were staying longer here in Pascal." Her tone was different. All the nervousness was gone.

Once the Struthers had left, Lucky asked his dad what had happened. Dad was running water in the little sink, getting ready to wash the dishes. "We had a good talk—opened up to each other some. Did you and Malcolm do the same?"

"Yeah. We had a nice chat and he told me to stay away from him and he'll do the same for me."

"Really? Did he say that?"

"Yes. He said white people act as if they want to be friends with blacks, but they don't really mean it."

Lucky's dad nodded a couple of times, but he was still looking down at the water. "Well, I think the parents feel mostly that way too, but they're at least trying to get beyond it."

"I don't get it, Dad. Are people mean to them or something?"

"No."

"What's the problem then?"

"They don't feel part of things—especially not at the branch."

"Maybe they won't let people be friends with them. Maybe they're like Malcolm."

"It's a lot more complicated than that, Lucky."

"I don't see why. He says whites don't want to be friends, but he's the one who tells me to stay away."

"Well, it isn't something that's easy to explain." He picked up a couple of plates and slid them into the sudsy water. "I guess there are some people in the branch who really don't want anything to do with them. The Struthers can deal with that. That's just plain old-fashioned prejudice. And then, a few of the people seem to be able to relax with them.

The parents have made friends with one Cajun family. They get along fine with them."

"So what about everyone else?"

"Well, there are things most of the people do—and probably don't know they're doing—that are hard to pin down."

"Like what, Dad? Give me an example."

"Well, Albert—Brother Struthers—told an interesting story. He said when he was in college—graduate school—he had a class from a professor who was really obnoxious to students. When he disagreed with them, he'd say, 'That's stupid. Where'd you get an idea like that?' But Albert noticed that the professor never said anything like that to him. He'd disagree, but he was always polite about it. So Albert started to go out of his way to say things he knew were wrong, just to test him."

"Wait a minute, Dad. I don't see what he was trying to do."

"He wanted to see if the guy had the guts to call him stupid. But he never did. He finally went to the professor's office and said, 'When I say something stupid, tell me. The same as anyone else.' But the guy never could do it."

Lucky sat down on his bed. "Dad, that doesn't make any sense to me."

"Well, Lucky, he wants people to forget what color he is and just treat him like any other person."

"I know. But if people are nice, that's a lot better than if they call him names."

"Yeah, it's better. But it's not equal."

"So what does he want—people at church to call him stupid?"

Dad laughed. "Well, not exactly," he said. "But that might be an improvement."

"It seemed to me that people at church treated them okay. Maybe they just have their minds made up—like Malcolm."

"It's hard to say. Let's watch on Sunday. Let's see whether you can pick up on anything."

"Okay," Lucky said, but he still didn't understand.

"And Lucky, hang in there with Malcolm. The Struthers told me he's gone through a very tough year down here."

"Yeah, I heard all about it."

"Lucky, just keep trying, okay? Treat him like a friend—no matter how he treats you. There's no place in the Church for racial prejudice. You know, when we call each other brother and sister, we're supposed to mean it."

"Dad, I already promised Malcolm that I'd stay away from him. That's what he wants from me."

"Well, that's one promise you shouldn't have made. It deserves to be broken."

"What're you talking about? My whole life you've been telling me I had to keep my promises."

Dad gave him a fake stare, as if he were really shocked. "You got to be kidding, Lucky. You don't really listen to me when I tell you stuff like that?"

"Hey, I do everything you tell me. I'm an obedient son."

"Okay, then. Here's the deal. Everything I tell you is wise, but some things are wiser than other things. And here's the wisest thing I'm going to tell you today: Forget the promise to Malcolm. Promise me you'll keep trying."

Lucky wasn't sure. He thought he'd rather keep the promise to Malcolm. But he said he'd do his best.

CHAPTER 7

The next morning the Pirates had another game. Lucky's father said he had to work, but he promised he'd make it to at least the second half. Lucky walked over a little early. As the guys started to arrive, he tried to be friendly. What he was looking for was someone who didn't seem to mind being friends with him. Big Carl was as nice as anyone, but he still treated Lucky like some stray dog he had found in the rain. Most of the guys started teasing immediately.

In the early part of the game, he stood on the sidelines watching, and no one paid much attention to him. Malcolm had a great first half, passing well, running well. The Rivermen, a team from a really small town named Renton, were pretty bad. They played hard, but no one could really keep up with Malcolm.

When Malcolm came to the sidelines, he talked, congratulated guys, laughed with them. He always seemed to be aware of himself, as though he knew that he was the star, but he wasn't that bad of a guy with his teammates.

Malcolm also kept his promise. He didn't razz Lucky, yet he didn't say a word to him either. Lucky was caught a little between promises. He didn't bother Malcolm, but once, when Malcolm came off the field, Lucky told him how well he was playing. He glanced at Lucky, but he didn't say anything.

In the second half, when the Pirates had built up a three-touchdown lead, the coach started putting in the substitute players. Eventually he got around to Lucky. "Okay, Lucky," he said, "Remember what I've been showing you about blocking. Tell Malcolm to run the seventeen option pass."

Lucky charged onto the field, yelling for Romaine to come out. He stepped to the huddle and said, "Seventeen option pass."

"Okay, but you'd better block for me." It sounded like a warning.

Lucky was nervous. When the center hiked the ball and Malcolm rolled to the right, Lucky remembered to go with the quarterback. Then, when the outside linebacker crashed past the Pirates' end, Lucky turned and put a shoulder into him. The guy put Lucky on the ground pretty hard and stumbled forward, but Lucky had slowed him long enough for Malcolm to get the pass away. It was complete for a short gain.

Lucky got up and looked toward Malcolm, hoping he'd seen that he had blocked the guy. "You're supposed to knock him down," he said. "He almost got to me."

Lucky nodded and trotted back to the huddle. He felt like telling Malcolm what he really thought. Romaine usually couldn't knock guys down either. Lucky had watched plenty. Romaine got in the way, slowed the tackler up long enough for Malcolm to get the pass off, and that seemed to be good enough for Malcolm.

The next play was a drop-back pass, and the result was much the same. Lucky met up with a linebacker. Lucky went down, but he managed to tangle himself up with the boy's legs enough to delay him, and Malcolm got the pass off. The pass was incomplete, however, and the linebacker pulled Malcolm's flag just after he had thrown the ball. More important, the guy had run right into Malcolm.

When Malcolm saw that the pass was over his receiver's head, he spun around to Lucky. "Come on, man. I got to have more time. It's no excuse you're little. If you can't play, you shouldn't be out here." Then, as though he had read Lucky's mind, "I'm not giving you a bad time. I'm just telling you how it is."

Yeah, right. The truth was, Malcolm had had enough time—he just hadn't thrown a good pass, and now he was blaming Lucky. Lucky didn't say anything though.

So it went for a time. The offense moved the ball fairly well, but nothing Lucky did was good enough.

Malcolm made a tough run for a first down near the ten-yard line, and things looked promising, but the next two plays went for about a yard. Then on third down, Lucky couldn't stop the rush. Two players got through the line, and Lucky lunged at one but had to let the other go by. One of the rushers got Malcolm's flag before he could throw the pass.

Malcolm was furious. In the huddle, he stared directly at Lucky and said, "You guys on the line can't let them get through like that because Lucky's useless. I might as well try to play alone back here."

"Hey, I—" But Lucky stopped.

Malcolm looked almost eager, as though he wanted to take whatever Lucky had to say and slam it back at him.

However, a new tight end ran onto the field. He

stepped into the huddle and called for a half-back sweep, with Lucky carrying the ball. Lucky gulped, but he liked the idea. He was mad and wanted to show Malcolm what he could do.

It was fourth down. He'd have to get all the way into the end zone or his team would turn the ball over. He was determined to do it—and show everybody.

For a moment, Malcolm stared at the player who'd brought in the call, then said, "No. That won't work. We're running I-19. I'll get the touchdown. You guys block for me. Lucky, block for once."

"Malcolm," Philip said, "we should do what the coach says."

"No. We want to score. Just block. I-19 on two."

Lucky was disappointed—and furious—yet he was also convinced that he'd knock someone flying. And he did give it his best shot. He ran toward a rusher as hard as he ever had but forgot everything he had been taught. He dove, out of control. The defender side-stepped, and Lucky flew on by, landing on his chest. When Lucky looked up, the guy he'd missed was forcing the play wide. Malcolm was running out of playing field as he approached the out-of-bounds line. He slowed and tried to find a place to turn up field, but three guys were coming up on him, and one of them got his flag.

Malcolm looked around and said, "Hey, great blocking. Thanks a lot." Then he turned and walked off the field with the rest of the offense.

But Coach Denton was coming toward him, walking down the sideline. "Malcolm, that wasn't the play I called."

"I know that. But I wanted to get the touchdown. Lucky never would have made it."

"That's not for you to decide, young man."

Malcolm stood in front of the coach with his hands on his hips, silent but defiant.

"You're coming out of the game." Coach Denton looked around at the other boys and shouted, "When we get the ball back, all the same guys go back in on offense, except Malcolm. Jud, I want you to play quarterback."

Malcolm walked away, but as he passed Lucky, he said, "Thanks a lot."

"Hey, Malcolm, you—"

Malcolm spun around so quickly that he frightened Lucky. "Go ahead and say it," he spat out.

Lucky could see Malcolm was ready for trouble. He wasn't sure anymore what he had been about to say, and now he knew, whatever it was, he'd better not. Lucky had just noticed that his dad was approaching the field. He had gotten there late, but he had kept his promise. Lucky knew he had to keep his promise too.

Lucky played the rest of the game. So did Jud. And it was a good thing the first team had built up such a large lead because the Pirate offense moved the ball very little—other than backwards—during the rest of the game. Once the Rivermen got some confidence, the rushers started crashing through on every play. Lucky got knocked down over and over. The only thing he knew for sure was that he got up the same number of times he went down, even though he thought he wouldn't make it a few times. Once, when the offense came off the field, his dad suggested that it might be time to ask the coach to let someone else play. Dirt and grass stains covered Lucky's sweats, and one cheek was streaked with mud. His knees had started giving way at times, so that when he walked, he'd suddenly have to catch himself from falling.

"I'm okay," he told his dad. "I'm just a little tired."

"Hey, Lucky," Robert called, "I think you hurt that guy. He bumped his knee against your head."

Lucky looked at his father. "See what I mean?"

"Don't worry about it," Dad said. "When you

get to be as big as that kid, he won't be able to touch you."

Lucky hoped that would be true. Only trouble was, he'd never see the guy again after another couple of weeks.

After the game, Dad said he had to hurry back to work. Lucky said it was okay. The coach wanted to talk to everyone, and then he would walk back to the RV.

"I can wait a minute and give you a ride."

"No. That's all right."

So Dad patted him on the back, told him how well he'd done. Lucky could have lived without that. No spot was left on his body that could take any of dad's "little" pats.

The coach chewed Malcolm out, of course. Then he told the guys that no one had played harder than Lucky. "You guys may make fun of him, but did you see him get up and get up, and just keep getting up?"

Winslow was right behind Lucky. He whispered, "To keep getting up, you have to keep getting knocked down." A couple of guys laughed, which made the coach all the angrier, but Lucky saw no sign that any of the boys were convinced. So, after the little speech, Lucky started the walk home alone. That was when he first noticed Sharon. She was sitting on a swing in the park playground, away from the field. Lucky thought very seriously of walking on by and pretending he hadn't seen her. He knew he would take some more guff from the guys if they saw him.

Sharon also seemed willing to let Lucky go by, but Lucky just couldn't do it. He changed course, walked over to the swings, and said, "Hi, Sharon. What are you doing?"

"I don't know. Jist sittin' here."

"Did you watch the game?"

"Some of it."

"Did you see me get smashed?"

"Yup. You okay?"

"Yeah. I'm tired though. And sore. Dad would say I'm lucky." He tried to smile.

"How come?"

"Well, he thinks . . . ah, never mind. How are things going with your house?"

"Perty good. It's 'most all cleared away. Papa says we can start buildin' again. Him 'n' my two big brothers'll build it."

"Did you get some insurance money?"

"Not yet. Papa says we ain't gittin' much. He's plannin' to jist make part of a house at first — and then put on some more later."

"Where are you living now?"

"With my aunt 'n' uncle. In town. It's crowded over there. Me 'n' my sisters sleep in my cousin's room, on the floor."

"That's kind of tough."

"It ain't so bad. I found some of my stuff too. I found my book, 'n' it wasn't tore up or anythin'. It jist got wet."

"What do you mean, your book?"

"I have a book. My grandma gave it to me."

"Just one?"

Sharon nodded. "Have you got lots of books?"

"Quite a few. What book do you have?"

"*The Secret Garden.* I've read it eight times. You ever read it?"

"No."

"You should. You could borrow mine sometime. It's good. Real good."

"You could read some of mine if you want. Don't you check out books from the library?"

Sharon shook her head.

"Why not?"

"I don't know. I guess I never thought on it."

"Do you have a library card?"

"What's that?"

"A card you can use to borrow books from the library. You should have one. If you want, we can

walk over there now and see what you have to do
to get one."

"That's okay."

"No. Come on."

Sharon shrugged and then stood up. She tow-
ered over Lucky. But the two of them walked from
the park—Lucky still covered with dirt, and Sharon
in an old, very worn pair of jeans. "Hey, Lucky's
with his girl," Winslow yelled. "Lucky, climb up a
tree and you'll be tall enough to kiss her."

Lucky and Sharon pretended they didn't hear.
They just kept walking.

"How come you want to play football?" Sharon
asked.

"I don't know. I thought it would be fun, I
guess."

"You're too little. You're going to get hurt."

"Not really. I just get banged around a little."

"I wouldn't play with those boys. They're too
mean to you."

"Yeah, probably. But if I quit, they'd just make
all the more fun of me."

"Yup. That's right. That's jist how they are.
They been teasing me my whole life."

"Don't let 'em bother you."

"I don't want to let 'em bother me. But they do
anyway. They jist do whether I say they do or not."

Yeah. Lucky understood that. But he soon understood it even better. He took a few more steps, then his knee suddenly buckled. He dropped to one knee and had to take a deep breath before he could get the strength to stand up again. Sharon stopped and looked at him. Then she reached out her hand to help him up.

Just as Lucky took her hand, Winslow bellowed, "Look at that. Lucky's proposing to Beanpole."

Lucky thought about crawling into a hole somewhere, but he couldn't see one, so he just stood up shakily and walked away. All the guys were still laughing.

CHAPTER 8

Lucky helped Sharon get a library card—or at least get the form her parents would have to sign—then went home and ached for a while. He thought about looking for bugs for his collection, but he just didn't feel like it. Mostly, he just rested until his dad came home.

"Hey, Lucky, come on out," his father yelled without even opening the door to the RV. "I bought a football. Let's practice."

"You got to be kidding," Lucky mumbled to himself.

"No, I'm not kidding. Come on."

How could Dad hear that? he wondered. Lucky got off his bed and limped outside. Ron Ladd was in a running-back stance: body bent forward, the football tucked under one arm, the other stretched forward and ready to stiff-arm all tacklers.

"Dad, I don't want to—"

"Now, look, Son, you need to benefit from my great knowledge of the game. I know you're a man in love, so it's hard to concentrate, but you need—"

"Dad, lay off. I'm not in love." He smiled though. How could Dad always make him do that?

"Okay, but you could still benefit from my instruction."

"But my body is one big bruise."

"Yeah, love does that to people."

"Dad!"

"Oh, yeah, sorry. Anyway, go out for a pass. I'll toss you a long one. You need to develop a few other facets of your game. Blocking may not be your greatest strength."

Lucky thought about returning to the RV, but he knew Dad wouldn't let him get away with that. So he hobbled away—which was as close as he could come to a run. His father threw him a pass, though it was to the wrong side, and Lucky couldn't adjust quickly enough. The ball hit him in the back of the head.

He stopped and turned around. "Dad, maybe some other time. I'm really not up to it right now."

"I'm sorry, Son," Dad said. "That was my fault. Toss the ball back, and we'll try again."

Lucky walked to the ball—slowly—picked it up, and gave it a looping toss. The football bounced well in front of Dad. But he chased after it, then pretended he was a quarterback. He took his "five-step drop," set himself, cocked his arm, and then yelled, "Go long!"

Lucky hobbled away again. The pass was over his head, but he picked up speed to get under it. All the same, the ball was beyond him. It struck the trunk of a big sycamore tree at the end of the parking lot . . . and bounced directly at Lucky. In self-defense, he screeched to a stop and brought up his hands, just as the ball struck him in the stomach. His feet flew out from under him, and he landed flat on his backside. The ball was in his arms.

"All right!" Dad yelled. "Great catch." He ran over to his son. "You're a natural."

Lucky thought he had no room for new pain, yet he was finding space for some.

"Are you okay?"

"No."

"Sure you are. Hey, that was some catch."

"Dad, that was an accident."

His father was grinning. "No way, Son. You've got instinct. You've got hands. My great hands. I knew you were my boy."

"Dad, I may never walk again. I think I broke something."

"Naw, I didn't hear any bones pop. You lucked out again. You landed on a good spot."

Lucky really tried hard this time. But he couldn't stop himself. He started to laugh, and dad's roar woke up people who were sleeping that time of day—in China.

The next morning, Lucky and his dad drove into Lafayette to church. On the way, Dad reminded Lucky that he wanted him to stay close to the Struthers to see how people treated them. "Is Malcolm still in Primary, or does he go to priesthood meeting?" Dad asked.

"Primary."

"Stick around him when you're in there. Just keep your eyes and ears open."

Lucky said he would try. "The thing is, I don't get what I'm watching for."

"Just see how people treat him. Ask yourself how you would feel about it."

"Don't say 'feel,' Dad. The only thing I can feel today is pain."

"Yeah, I guess that's true. Love is like that."

"*Dad!*"

Lucky and his dad arrived a little early. Lucky was so sore he could hardly get out of the RV. He would have limped, but it was hard to limp with both legs, so he lurched. Since standing was easier than sitting, he welcomed the chance to stand in the foyer while Dad chatted with Brother Giles. About five minutes before the meeting started, the Struthers came in. Dad went over and said hello to them. They seemed happy to see him.

Brother Giles walked over too. "Brother Struthers, Sister Struthers, it's sure good to see you. How are you?"

Brother Giles smiled and shook hands with both hands — the whole business. Lucky couldn't see anything bad about that.

"How's your work going?"

"Oh, fine. It's just a little busier than I'd like. I end up putting in some long days."

"Do you? Well, that's too bad. I guess that's what comes with being such an important man."

"Well, I'm not —

"And Malcolm, how's school going? I hear you're the star of the football team."

Malcolm shrugged and looked away.

"Now isn't that right, Sister Struthers? He's some athlete, from what I hear."

"He does really well," she said politely.

Brother Giles was going overboard to be nice — smiling more than usual and sounding nervous.

Lucky could see what the Struthers meant, maybe. He could also tell that Brother Giles meant well.

Then the others began. Almost everyone who came through the foyer said hello to Dad and Brother Giles and the Struthers, yet Lucky could see a difference, an extra something that the members put into their greetings when they talked to the Struthers—and they did seem sort of awkward about it. Was that so awful though?

Lucky waited until Malcolm walked into the little multipurpose room where Primary was held, then followed him in and sat on another row, behind Malcolm. He didn't dare say anything. He was also rather preoccupied with his own pain—he had just put the sorest part of his body on a hard chair.

In a moment the Primary president, Sister Doxey, came over and reached out her hand to Malcolm. "Good morning, Malcolm. How are you?" He shook her hand but didn't say anything.

"Well, now, you're not looking very cheery this morning." She smiled brightly and cocked her head to one side. "Are you feeling all right, Malcolm?"

"Yeah. I'm fine."

"Well, good. I hope you have a nice time at Primary this morning. You know, I think you're a very special boy."

Okay. Lucky knew that was a bit much—but Primary presidents were like that.

She came over to Lucky next. "And this is our new boy—Lucky. How are you this morning? All ready for Primary?"

Lucky nodded. "Sure," he said. What he was really thinking was that he couldn't wait for his birthday that winter, so he could move on to priesthood.

After Primary and before sacrament meeting, Dad chatted a little with the Struthers. When everyone went into the chapel, Lucky took the chance to whisper in his dad's ear, "Everybody was nice to them. Maybe they're a little too nice sometimes—but that doesn't seem so bad to me." The Struthers, just a little ahead of them, sat down, and Lucky and his dad joined them.

Dad nodded, then whispered, "Okay. Well, keep watching. Try to think how you'd feel. I saw some of what they're talking about. It's kind of subtle, and I think it's harder for us to pick up on than it is for them."

Lucky did notice something different happen. The Struthers' friends—a Cajun family Lucky hadn't met before—came by and chatted with Brother and Sister Struthers. The man even teased them about dressing up so fancy. He didn't seem to be worried about offending them, and the Struthers didn't seem bothered either. It was something for Lucky to think about.

After the meeting, Dad walked out with the Struthers. When they reached the foyer, he said, "Are you planning to go to the branch Halloween party?"

"I don't know," Sister Struthers said, and she glanced at her husband, as though unsure.

"I wish you would," Dad said. "You could go with Lucky and me."

"I've never been much for costumes and all that sort of thing," Brother Struthers said.

"Don't wear one. I probably won't. But I have something the boys could wear. They'd have a lot of fun."

Lucky saw Malcolm shoot a rather desperate look at his dad. "Well, I really would like to see the boys have a good time . . . together. Yes, maybe we ought to do that."

"Great. Just stop over at our RV on the way. We'll suit Malcolm up."

Lucky caught one last look from Malcolm before the Struthers left. Malcolm was not pleased, and his look seemed to say that part of the reason was that he didn't want to be around Lucky.

All that didn't bother Lucky anymore. That was

to be expected. But something else was confusing. Dad didn't have any costumes. Lucky knew every article they carried around with them in their motor home, and one thing they didn't have was any sort of Halloween costume. What was he up to?

On Halloween, Dad came home with a box, and when the Struthers came by, he opened it up and pulled out two very fancy costumes. One was a panda bear, with a huge head on it. He gave that one to Lucky. Then he said to Malcolm, "I hope you don't mind being a chicken, but this one will fit you better." The costume was a lot like the one the famous baseball chicken always wore. Lucky started pulling on his bear suit over his clothes. He figured Dad didn't want him to ask where it had come from, not in front of the Struthers.

Malcolm held his suit in front of him, looking it over. "Mr. Ladd," he said politely, "I think I'd rather just not wear a costume."

Before Dad could answer, Brother Struthers said, "Nonsense, Malcolm. That's a terrific outfit. Put it on."

"Why?" Lucky could see the controlled rage in Malcolm's eyes.

"Well, why not? What's the problem? Don't you want to be a chicken?"

"I just don't want to wear a costume. You're not wearing one; I don't see why I have to."

"All the kids are going to wear costumes. Now come on. Don't be a bad sport."

Sister Struthers patted her son on the shoulder. "Come on, Malcolm. It'll be fun."

"Mama, I don't want to."

"Just put it on," Brother Struthers said. He was starting to sound angry.

"I don't see why I have to—"

"Okay, fine," his dad said. "Take your pick. That or your next football game. You put it on right now, or you're grounded for a week, and that means missing your game."

It was an awkward moment. Malcolm looked mad enough to consider missing the game, but he kept his control enough to think about it first.

"Look, Malcolm," Brother Ladd said, "why don't you try it on, and we'll go over to the party. If you're not having any fun, we won't stay long. In fact, here's an idea that might make it especially fun: why don't you and Lucky just make animal noises—growls and clucks—and see whether anyone can figure out who you are."

"That'll be fun, honey," Sister Struthers said. "Give it a try."

Malcolm was giving way. Lucky figured he liked

the idea of not having to talk. "How long do we have to stay?" he asked.

"Not long," his father said. "I still have some work I have to get done when we get home."

So Malcolm pulled on the suit. It had a fat middle and came with floppy shoe coverings that looked like chicken feet. Lucky's suit had a huge head that made Lucky look much taller than usual. In fact, the two boys looked about the same height once they were all suited up.

Sister Struthers was the first to laugh, but Brother Struthers also got a kick out of the way the boys looked. He was relaxing around Dad more all the time. "I never thought I'd raise such a fine-looking chicken," he told Lucky's father.

"You guys look great," Dad said. "I'll bet those are the best two costumes at the party."

Lucky didn't doubt that, but he still wondered what was going on. He knew his dad, and his dad was up to something.

"Okay, now remember. No words at all. Just growl, Lucky, and Malcolm, you make clucking noises. We won't even walk in with you, and we'll see how long it takes before people figure out who you are."

"I don't think we can get them in the car with those things on," Brother Struthers said.

"I know. I already thought of that. Just sit down, and we'll drive our house over."

Everyone laughed. Everyone except Malcolm.

When Dad started up the RV, and Lucky took the seat up front, next to him, Dad whispered, "Tonight's your chance to see what it's like to be Malcolm."

CHAPTER 9

*T*he party was being held at one of the member's homes—in a large recreation room. When the boys walked in, they got a big reaction, as Lucky thought they probably would. A man who was greeting people said, "My goodness, who's this?" Lucky gave him a big growl, but the chicken was silent.

Once inside, a number of kids surrounded the boys immediately. "Who's in there?" one little boy kept asking. Lucky roared, and Malcolm stepped back a little.

So it went for a time. Lucky was having rather a good time, and people kept guessing that he was almost everyone but himself—probably because he looked so tall. Then his dad and the Struthers came walking in, and Lucky decided to throw the guessers off by growling at them. He gave his dad a big roar, and Dad acted like he was about to fall down. "Who in the world is that?" he asked, loud enough for almost everyone to hear.

Lucky laughed inside his suit and turned to walk away. Just then, he overheard his dad say to someone, "That's actually the Struthers boy—Malcolm."

Lucky stopped and looked around. He thought maybe Dad was pointing across the room. His father, however, was talking to a man in the branch presidency—Carruthers, or something like that. The man nodded and said, "Hey, Malcolm, you're looking good."

In the next few minutes, the secret seemed to get all around. Lucky thought Dad was spreading it. Several other people, even some of the kids, began to call him Malcolm.

Things were starting to get organized now. Sister Doxey announced that a game of musical chairs was about to begin. Some of the members helped arrange the chairs, and the kids started lining up. Malcolm was leaning against a wall nearby, but he didn't walk out to join the game, even when Sister Doxey asked him to.

Lucky saw a little boy, about four years old, walk up to Malcolm. "Hey, chicken," he said. Malcolm didn't respond; he didn't even seem to notice the boy.

"Hey, chicken," the little boy shouted louder, "can't you talk?"

Malcolm finally looked down.

"Chicken. Chicken." Then the little boy grabbed the arm of the suit—the wing—and gave it a hard pull. Suddenly Malcolm's arm lashed out, catching the little boy on the shoulder. The boy seemed to take that for fun, though, and came back grabbing. This time Malcolm pushed against the boy's chest fairly hard and sent the boy stumbling backwards.

A young woman—the mother, Lucky supposed—hurried over to the little boy and picked him up. "Mikey, you're okay," she assured him, then looked at Malcolm. "That wasn't necessary, Lucky," she said, sharply and sternly. "You didn't have to push him like that. He's just a little boy."

Lucky cringed. Malcolm was mad enough as it was without someone getting on him like that—even if she thought he was someone else. Yet that made Lucky wonder. What if she had known it was Malcolm? Would she have acted the same way?

The game was beginning, but Lucky decided not to join. He had another idea. He walked nearer to the woman with the little boy. She had just set him back down, and he was already looking around for something else to do.

Lucky had only to give the boy a little roar to get his attention.

"Hey, bear," the boy said, "you're ugly." He slugged Lucky in the soft belly of his costume.

Lucky roared again, and the little boy laughed. "I'll kick you, bear," he said and gave Lucky a pretty good shot in the leg.

Lucky cringed. His first thought was to ask the boy not to do that, then he realized that this was his chance to find something out. He reached down, gave the little guy a pretty good shove, and in a low voice said, "Get away from me, you little brat." He looked to see if the boy's mother could hear. She stepped toward them, but as Lucky looked at her, she hesitated, as though she were unsure what she wanted to do.

The boy quickly came back for more. This time Lucky roared as loudly as he could, hoping to draw attention, and gave the boy a swat with the back of his paw.

"Stop that, bear," the little boy said, but he wasn't hurt. Lucky looked around. He could see that quite a few people were watching. The little boy's mother was still waiting. "Mikey," she said, "don't do that. Come here."

"I'm going to eat you, bear," the little boy said, and he flung himself at Lucky's legs. Lucky grabbed

him and threw him back, hard—even harder than
he had intended. The little boy landed on his seat
and started to howl.

Lucky looked at the mother again. She hurried
to her little son and reached down to pick him up.
"Mikey, you shouldn't do that," she said. She held
him close and patted him on the back. "Come on.
You're all right." Then she looked at the bear. "I'm
sorry, Malcolm," she said, not very convincingly.

This was crazy, but Lucky thought he understood. Now he wanted to try something else. Lucky
strode across the room to Malcolm. "Bears eat
chickens," he said softly, so only the two could hear.
Then he growled loud enough to attract the attention of everyone in the room and lunged at the
chicken. Malcolm was taken by surprise. "What do
you think you're doing?" he said. Again Lucky
slammed into him hard, putting a shoulder into him
the way he blocked on the football field, but now
Malcolm was ready and shoved back. "You're going
to get it," Malcolm said.

Lucky stepped back, growled, and drove himself
forward, slamming into Malcolm again. Malcolm
came back with the same kind of force, but his big
costume was in the way. Lucky jumped back and
got ready to attack once again when he finally heard
someone coming. A hand was suddenly placed on

his shoulder, pulling him back, and then Brother Giles jumped in between the two of them. He looked squarely at Malcolm. "Lucky, you know better than to act like that. That's way out of line."

Now Lucky knew for sure.

Malcolm said, "I'm not Lucky," and, at the same time, Lucky reached up to pull some Velcro loose and pulled off his big head.

"I'm Lucky."

Brother Giles spun around. He looked confused. "What?"

"That's Malcolm. You finally figured it out. Go ahead and take your head off, Malcolm."

Brother Giles stepped back. Lucky saw him glance around at the people. Everyone was watching, and the room was quiet. Malcolm pulled off his chicken head.

"I don't understand this, Lucky," Brother Giles said. "What were you trying to do?"

"You said it was his fault," Lucky said, pointing to Malcolm.

"Well, you were the one who started the pushing."

"That's not what you said just a minute ago. How come you're switching around?"

"Well, I . . . wasn't sure . . . I don't want to hurt

anyone's feelings here. You understand that, don't you?"

Lucky knew exactly what he meant. He looked at Malcolm, even stepped past Brother Giles. "I understand now," he said. "I can see why you don't like coming here."

Malcolm wasn't listening. "I'm going to bust you up at our next practice," he said.

"Now, boys, let's not have any hard feelings," Brother Giles said. "I think maybe Lucky just got carried away a little with his bear act. Malcolm, you were just defending yourself. Let's not be upset by any of this."

Lucky's father and Brother Struthers walked across the room. "Malcolm," Brother Struthers said. "What in the world were you two doing?"

"He started pushing me."

"Lucky was the one who really did the pushing," Brother Giles said. "I think he was just playing, but he let it get a little out of hand. I'm sure no one meant any harm."

"Brother Giles," Lucky said, "don't you see what you did? Can't you see what's happening around here? You blamed it on Malcolm when we had our masks on. Now you're blaming it on me."

"Lucky, why don't you just apologize? I think

that would be the best way to settle this." Lucky could see how embarrassed he was.

Lucky didn't mind apologizing, but he wanted everyone to understand—especially Malcolm. The trouble was, Malcolm had already made up his mind what he thought of the whole thing. He reached out and grabbed Lucky by the fabric of his big suit. "I'm going to get you," he said, then walked away, heading out of the room.

Lucky looked around. "Can't you see what just happened?" he said to anyone who would listen. He glanced at his dad, who just shook his head.

Then he heard a woman say, "Oh, dear. I hope Malcolm didn't get his feelings hurt. I've been afraid of something like that."

"You don't treat Malcolm the same as other people—just because he's black," Lucky said.

The room suddenly went silent. No one would even look at Lucky. Finally Brother Giles said, "Lucky, that's enough." He turned to Brother Struthers and said, "I'm really sorry about this."

Lucky looked around at everyone. He thought hard about how to explain. But no one wanted to hear him. They were too embarrassed. No one would even make eye contact.

Lucky felt his dad's hand on his shoulder. "Well, now you understand," he said.

"Yeah, but I'm the only one."

Later that night, after they had driven a very quiet Struthers family back to their car and the Struthers had returned home, Lucky and his dad talked. They tried to think what to do. "Ask yourself this," his father said. "What would you want, if you were Malcolm?"

"I don't know exactly," Lucky said. "That's what I've been trying to decide. When those people were all grinning at me and treating me as if they were afraid of me, I just wanted to tell them to lay off. They seemed so phony."

Dad sat at the table, leaning forward. He had been eating a bowl of ice cream, but now he just stared down at the table. "That's what Malcolm's sick of," he said.

"When I told him I wanted to be friends, he didn't trust me, did he?" Lucky was polishing off the last of his Rocky Road ice cream. He thought of Malcolm saying his real friends were black.

"So, what're you going to do?" Dad asked.

"I don't know."

"You'll think of something."

"Can't you help me?"

"Well, I will say this. I think Malcolm has been pushing you on purpose. I think he wants to find out whether you'll ever stand up to him—the way you would if a white kid was doing the same thing. Remember that professor who wouldn't tell Malcolm's dad that he was stupid?"

"Yeah."

"I'd give that some thought."

"I don't think I want to tell Malcolm he's stupid. He might smash me."

"Yeah, that's one possible outcome." A smile slipped into Dad's eyes. He said, in a very serious tone, "I'd hate to see you get smashed. You wouldn't look good that way. And I hate to think what that would do to Tiffany. Her poor heart would be broken."

"Dad."

"Okay, okay. You're not in love. You already told me."

"That's right."

"But I'd say you're in some pretty serious like at this stage."

"Dad, we're talking about Malcolm."

"All right, I know. If my theory is wrong, he just might smash you. Do you feel like taking the chance?"

"I don't know. I'll think about it."

CHAPTER 10

*T*he next morning Lucky decided he'd try talking to Malcolm. He thought maybe he could explain everything now. Maybe that would be a better approach than doing anything . . . drastic.

He saw Malcolm outside the school with Winslow. Lucky walked up and was about to say something when Malcolm said, "My dad told me that if I do anything to you, he won't let me play football the rest of the season."

"Malcolm, come on. Don't you understand what I was trying to do?"

"You were trying to get your head knocked off."

"Malcolm's dad didn't tell me to lay off you," Winslow said. "I can bust your head."

Lucky knew better than to say anything else. Malcolm wasn't going to listen right now—not with Winslow around.

Lucky thought a lot that morning. Maybe his dad's way was the only way. By recess, he had hatched a plan—but he knew he was taking a very big risk.

When recess came, Lucky went outside and found Sharon. She was in her usual place, on the monkey bars—not playing but just sitting. "Hi, Sharon."

"Hey."

Lucky laughed. "How come you say hey instead of hi?"

"How come you say hi instead of hey?" She laughed too.

"How're you doing anyway?"

"Okay."

"How come you don't ever do anything with the girls?"

Sharon looked at the ground. "I don't know. The boys tease me; the girls don't, mostly. But they don't talk to me much neither. That's all I know."

Lucky leaned against one of the bars in front of Sharon. "Don't you have someone you can talk to, or do things with?"

"My one sister, sort of."

"No one else?"

"Nope."

"You ought to make friends with someone, Sharon."

She was still looking down. She shrugged and said, "That's what Mama tells me."

"She's right, Sharon. If you just sit over here every day, you won't ever have any friends."

Sharon didn't answer. She let her chin rest on her arm. He was sorry he had said anything. "All I mean is—you can't make friends if you stay away from everybody."

Sharon still didn't speak. She seemed not to be listening. Then she surprised Lucky. "How soon you leavin'?" she asked and looked right at him.

"Next week probably. Maybe two weeks. I'm not sure."

"Where do you go next?"

"I don't know. We'll stay here longer if nothing happens that we have to hurry off to."

She looked away again, sat quietly for a time, and then said, "I wish I could go someplace sometime."

"Where?"

"I don't know. I never seen any other places."

"Haven't you ever been out of Louisiana?"

"I never even been out of . . . right around here."

"You haven't been to Baton Rouge, or New Orleans, or—"

"Nope."

That was hard for Lucky to imagine. "There's lots of stuff to see," he said. "But this is a nice place to live."

"I guess it is. I wouldn't want to move all the time, like you. But I want to see something else." She smiled a little, although her eyes didn't change. "Maybe someday I'll get in an airplane and fly somewheres. Paris, France, or somewheres like that."

"Yeah. I'd like to do that too. I flew in an airplane only once. We usually drive everywhere."

"That'd be okay too, I guess."

Lucky nodded. He still had a plan. "Let's go for a little trip now. Let's walk around the playground."

Sharon raised her head, and Lucky saw her eyes widen. "What for?"

"Just for a walk."

"Them boys over there will tease us like you never heard before."

"Naw. I've heard everything they've got to say."

Sharon wasn't moving. "I don't want to," she said. "I don't want ever'body lookin' at us. Ever'one will say you're my boyfriend."

"Just laugh if they do. It doesn't matter."

"Naw. I don't think so."

"Come on. You need some exercise. You've been sitting around too much."

She was still saying no, but she was sliding out of the monkey bars, and she had started to laugh. "I don't guess I will," she said, but Lucky saw something new in her eyes.

"Come on."

"You ain't tryin' to be my boyfriend, are you?"

"No. We're just friends."

"But you're a boy."

"That's okay. I can't help it." He laughed, and so did she. Then Lucky started walking, and she quickly caught up.

"Where we goin'?"

"I don't know," Lucky said, but that was not true. He was heading toward the fence so they could make a loop around the playground, and he had in mind to walk directly past Malcolm and the other boys.

"I bet we look funny," Sharon said.

"Why?"

"You know why."

"Hey, if you mean because you're taller than I am, don't worry about it. Everybody is. That's nothing new."

Lucky watched the boys. As he and Sharon came

nearer, Winslow pointed at them and said something to the other guys. The football game came to a halt. The abuse began.

"Let's go the other way," Sharon said.

"Naw. We don't care what they say."

Sharon laughed, but nervously. "They're goin' to say I'm your girlfriend. You watch."

"That's okay."

But the guys didn't come up with anything that kind. "Lucky, what's that you got with you — a giraffe?" Winslow yelled.

Lucky looked at Sharon. Suddenly she wasn't laughing. "Come on. Let's go the other way," she said.

"Giraffes are beautiful," Lucky said. "That guy's probably trying to give you a compliment."

"No, he ain't. Let's go."

"He's afraid to play football. That's why he has to hang around with a girl." This was from Malcolm. Lucky took several more steps to get fairly close to the guys, then said, "Malcolm, shut your mouth."

Lucky saw the reaction. All the guys were stunned. Malcolm seemed not to believe what he had heard. He walked toward Lucky, slowly, his eyes aimed like gun sights. "What did you say?"

Lucky knew exactly what he was going to say.

He had planned it all ahead of time. "I told you to shut your mouth. What you just said was stupid."

"Are you calling me stupid?"

"Yes. At least you're acting that way."

Malcolm and Lucky had come face to face now. Sharon stopped and backed away. "You think I won't pound you, just because you're so little — and because of my dad. That's the only reason you have the guts to say that to me."

"Malcolm, I thought you had some brains, but maybe you don't."

Malcolm doubled up his fists, held them as though he were ready to knock Lucky down, but that's not what Lucky saw in his eyes. The football players behind Malcolm seemed to hold their breaths. Lucky and Malcolm stared into each other's eyes. It was not a time to blink. Lucky kept watching, waiting. What he didn't see was any anger. He thought maybe Malcolm was trying to decide how to react.

Finally Winslow stepped up and said, "Get him, Malcolm. Or I will." Big Carl, who stood just behind Winslow, shook his head slowly, as though he now expected the worst. Malcolm kept watching Lucky. He still seemed unsure of himself.

"Come on, Malcolm, knock him flat."

"Go ahead and knock me down, Malcolm. I'll just get up and tell you what I think of you."

"So go ahead and tell me."

It was a strange thing to ask, and Malcolm actually sounded curious. Luckily, Lucky knew what he wanted to say. "For one thing, you treat Sharon rotten — all you guys do — and the only thing she ever did was grow tall." Malcolm's eyes dropped, avoided Lucky's. "If someone teased you about being black, you'd knock him across the street. Maybe that's what somebody ought to do to you."

The whole world seemed to take a breath. Lucky had never heard such silence. Malcolm didn't react, didn't even move.

"Another thing. You don't have any right to make up your mind about me just because I'm white."

"Who said I did?"

"You told me how things are. Well, I don't think they're always that way. You don't have any right to hate me because I'm white."

"Maybe I don't. Maybe I don't like you because you're such a cocky little runt."

"No way. I'm not half as cocky as you are, and you know it."

Then something strange happened. Malcolm smiled for a second — just barely, but Lucky caught it. "Maybe I got a right to be cocky," he said. "Maybe you don't."

"Hey, you're good at sports. But there's a lot of other stuff in this world."

Winslow was the one who was bristling and pounding his fist into his hand, but Malcolm was listening. "So what's the deal then? You don't like me?" He actually laughed just a little.

"I don't know. I don't know you."

"Do you think I care either way?"

"Probably not, but . . . yeah, I think you care."

"Why should I?"

Lucky looked away for a few seconds. All the guys had crowded close around Malcolm, and Winslow said, "Don't talk to him. Shut his mouth for him."

By then, Lucky knew what he wanted to say. "I think you want a real friend. You're sick of these guys who follow you around like a bunch of dough-heads, just because you're so good at sports. You're sick of white people who think they have to be careful around you all the time. You'd rather have somebody tell you the truth when you're acting like a jerk."

"If I want a friend, it won't be some cocky little shrimp like you." Those were only the words, though. That little smile was there again. He and

Lucky both knew the words meant something else. All the same, he turned and tried to leave. The guys began to step away to give him room.

"You just lucked out, man," Winslow said. "Malcolm's in a good mood, or he would've killed you."

"Oh, lay off, Winslow. Why do you have to act so tough all the time?"

"Look, Lucky," Winslow said and took hold of Lucky's shirt. "I may not be in as good a mood as Malcolm is."

"Leave him alone, Winslow." Everyone looked at Malcolm, who had turned around and pointed a finger at Winslow. "Let go of him. Come on, let's go."

Winslow shrugged, looking sort of embarrassed, but he followed after Malcolm. The other guys trailed after both of them.

Lucky stood alone for a moment, then rejoined Sharon. She shook her head slowly. "I don't believe you did that. You must've lost your mind."

"Not me. I planned it ahead of time." Then he added, "But I don't believe I did it either. I was shaking clear down to my shoes."

"You're nuts. He's goin' to get you—sooner or later."

"Nope. I don't think so. I think we're going to be friends now."

"Lucky, what're you talkin' about? You can't make friends by tellin' some guy he's stupid."

"Well, that's a good point." Lucky laughed. "It's a special method. It wouldn't work on just anybody."

CHAPTER 11

*T*he boys had another game on Saturday. Lucky didn't play at first. Once again, though, the team built up a good lead, and shortly after the half, Coach Denton sent Lucky in. When he entered the huddle, Malcolm said, "You'd better be ready to block today." The words were more or less the same, but the tone was different enough that Lucky knew something had changed between them.

The other team—the St. Martin Saints—wasn't really very good, but they did have a couple of big defensive linemen. Malcolm called a pass on the very first play, and the rushers came hard. The line held up at first, but a big kid broke through, and Lucky stepped in front of him. He drove his shoulder into the guy's middle, but a knee caught Lucky in the midsection, and another one hit him in the

shoulder as he was going down. Lucky ended up
flat on his back.

For a moment, things were swirling—both the
players and the little stars in his head. Lucky
thought he had started getting up almost immediately, but he noticed, when he was finally on his
feet, that the players on his team had collected
around him. "Did you get the pass off?" Lucky
asked.

"Yeah," Malcolm said. "But Philip dropped it.
Are you okay?"

"Sure. Let's go get 'em."

"Right," Robert said. "You'd better get a two-
by-four if you're going to block that guy."

"Shut up, Robert," Malcolm said. "Lucky can
block him."

Everyone moved over a few steps and formed
their huddle. Lucky was still not in total contact
with what was going on, but he didn't want to leave
the game. The next couple of plays went better,
however. The line stopped the rush. Lucky pre-
pared to block but didn't have to. Malcolm missed
on the next pass. Then on third down, he threw to
Philip again, who caught it this time and broke loose
for a long run. Suddenly the Pirates had first down
on the fifteen-yard line, and they were in a good
position to score.

Lucky hurried forward with the rest of his team, and everyone slapped hands with Philip. Just as the team was getting into its huddle again, a player ran onto the field. He yelled for one of the guards to come out, then told Malcolm, "The coach says I-29 pitchout and block."

"Okay," Malcolm said and grinned. "Let's see if Lucky's as good as he thinks he is. Let's all block for him."

Lucky felt his stomach do a flip-flop, but he was excited more than scared. This was his big chance. As he walked up to the line, he thought, *The other team knows I'm getting the ball. It's so obvious. How can they help but see it in my face?* He assumed his stance, listened to the count, and then, as the center hiked the ball, cut to the right. He watched Malcolm and got ready for the pitch.

Things were setting up. Lucky saw the pulling guard sweep to the right. He just needed the ball now. Then it was on its way, right into his hands. And Lucky was on his way too. He sprinted as hard as he could around the right end. But a defender had gotten by the blockers and was coming at Lucky fast. Lucky put on the brakes and jumped to the side just in time. The guy grabbed for his flag and missed.

Lucky tried to run to the right again, the way

the play had been planned, but the defense had had time to pursue in that direction. Everything was closed off. He pulled up, slipped a little on the grass, then cut back to the left. Another defensive player streaked across the field toward him but lost his balance when Lucky cut back. He lunged at the flag as he fell, just missing it. Lucky was racing at full speed now to the left and picking up blockers.

He thought he saw room to go all the way, angling left across the field and squeezing into the left corner of the end zone. He thought for a moment that he might make it, but some of the Saints were faster, and they started to cut off his angle. His blockers needed to knock some guys out of the way for Lucky to get in.

Lucky ran hard, but as he neared the sideline, he slowed to give his blockers a chance to help. If they could stop a couple of guys, he could dive into the corner. However, all the players were on a collision course, and when they came together, Lucky heard bodies smack and saw a confusion of arms and legs. He glimpsed a bit of an opening, though, and darted toward the corner at the same moment a defender broke through the blockers. The boy reached for the flag, but his momentum carried him right into Lucky.

Wham! Lucky was suddenly airborne. He didn't

know whether he had crossed the goal line, didn't know whether the guy had got his flag, wasn't even sure that he still had the ball in his arms. He landed on his neck and shoulders, flipped over backwards, and came down on his face. He was okay, he told himself, and started to get up. At least, that was the signal his brain sent to his body: "Get up. Go ahead. Right now. Just start moving your arms and legs, and get up."

He didn't think the idea was working though. Too much grass was still in his face. If he had been getting up, that stuff should be gone by now. Then someone grabbed him around the middle and set him upright. Lucky felt earth under his feet; he just couldn't see. "Did I make it?" he gasped.

"Not quite. You went out of bounds on the one-yard line. We'll get it on this next play."

"Right." Lucky made his legs move, but not so well as he would have liked, because grass was suddenly in his face again. This time two guys helped him up—one on each side.

"Lucky, are you okay?"

"Yeah, sure." And it was true. He was walking fine, except that his feet dragged, and guys had to hold him up by the arms, pulling him.

Suddenly Malcolm stood in front of him.

"Lucky, you still want to get the touchdown, don't you? Can you carry the ball again?"

"Sure. Where is it?"

"What?"

Lucky tried to take actual steps now. The guys let go, and he stumbled into the huddle, tripped, and fell. As he started to get up, he said, "Malcolm, you run it in. I'll block. I'm not exactly sure which way we're going." And then, strangely, the grass came up and hit him in the knees, found its way to his chest, and smacked him pretty hard in the face. Lucky decided to rest there for just a minute.

When Lucky woke up, he was lying on the sidelines, Coach Denton looking down at him. "Can you see me?" he was asking, and Lucky realized the coach had asked that a couple of times before.

"Yup. You look as bad as ever."

After the laughing quieted down, Coach Denton patted Lucky on the chest and said, "Just stay there for a minute." Lucky had been trying to get up again. "I'll tell you what, son. I think you're the toughest kid I ever coached. I want you to know that."

"Did Malcolm get the touchdown?"

"No. Romaine did. But you would have."

Lucky wished it had happened that way. He had really wanted that touchdown. He was seeing better now, and all the guys on the offense were looking down at him. Malcolm said, "Good job, Lucky."

Then the others joined in. "Great run," one of the players said. Lucky would have sworn it was Winslow.

The next day on the way to church, Lucky told his dad he liked football, but he wasn't sure playing the games on Saturdays was such a good idea. "I won't have a place on me I can sit down on until at least Tuesday, and those benches at church are pretty hard." Brother Ladd let out one of his shake-the-RV laughs.

Lucky was exaggerating, but just barely. He got through Primary all right by sitting softly—and not moving much. Malcolm sat next to him. They really didn't say much. Malcolm seemed a little embarrassed, and Lucky didn't know what to talk about.

When Lucky came into the chapel for fast-and-testimony meeting, he discovered that his dad had gone out to the RV and brought in a cushion. He pointed and grinned, and Lucky laughed, but he was thankful all the same.

Dad leaned over and whispered, "I talked to my quorum about helping out Sharon's family. A couple of the men know the family, but they didn't know quite how things stood. They said they'd get something organized this week. One of the brothers has the kind of power tools that the Talbots probably don't have, and another said he thought he could save them a lot of money on materials—he works for a lumber company."

"That's good, Dad. Really good."

"Maybe the two of us can go over and help some—until we have to leave."

"Okay. I'd like to."

Lucky was pleased though not surprised. But what Dad did during the meeting was definitely surprising. He was the very first person to get up and bear his testimony. The chapel was small enough that the people didn't have to use a microphone, and Dad's voice was loud enough that he didn't need one anyway. However, he talked rather softly today. He and Lucky were toward the front of the chapel, so Brother Ladd turned around, pushing his hands down into his pockets.

"There's something I feel I've got to explain to you," he said to the congregation. "Lucky and I will be leaving soon—maybe even before next Sunday. So this might be the only chance I'll get."

Lucky wondered what his dad was talking about. This wasn't at all like him. "Lucky tried to show you all something at the Halloween party the other night, but I'm not sure you caught on. It's really as simple as this: you're being way too nice to the Struthers family."

Lucky felt the quiet come into the room. Dad seemed to sense that he had gotten everyone's attention too. He let a little time pass. "Now that might sound strange. But I think what's happening is that you're all so concerned about proving you're not prejudiced that you go out of your way to be super nice to them. That might seem okay on the surface, but what happens is that they feel very uncomfortable.

"Being nice is fine, but when you exaggerate the whole thing, you make them feel different from everyone else . . . sort of separated. And that's what they don't need. They want to be brothers and sisters with you. They don't want to be the nice black family in the branch. They just want to be people, the same as everyone else. I think what happens, too, is that the Struthers start to wonder what you're really thinking. It's like you're hiding something if you can't just treat them like anyone else. It's hard for them to trust you."

Lucky was glad that Dad had said it, but he didn't know what everyone would think. Maybe they wouldn't understand. They sure hadn't understood at the party. Dad bore his testimony of the gospel, thanked the good people for their kindness to him and Lucky, and sat down.

The room remained silent for a long time, and no one stood up. Then Lucky heard a voice he knew: that controlled voice of Brother Struthers, still deep and round but shaking. "I want to thank Brother Ladd. He does understand. We joined the Church because we believed it was true, and we went to a ward in Chicago that had quite a number of black families. We just didn't have any sense that we were . . . different. It's been difficult for us here, but not because you haven't tried very hard to do what's right. We would merely like to get beyond that now. I hope you understand."

He stood there for a moment, silent, and Lucky had the feeling he was trying to find just the right words. "When I'm among people of my own race, I feel comfortable, so I find myself drawn to them. Around whites, I often feel a little out of place. Yet my whole life I've been longing to be . . . a person. Not a black person—just a person. Not a black Mormon—just a Mormon. Can you understand that?

"I'm most worried about my son, Malcolm. Right now he's trying to find a place—just figure out where he belongs. It's hard for him to trust people who say they accept him but don't seem to mean it. I want him to accept the Church, but I think—first—you have to accept him. That means just treat him like you would any other boy who meets with you each Sunday."

Once he sat down, others began to stand, and many mentioned that they knew they'd made mistakes in dealing with the Struthers. One older man, a local man who said he had joined the church a couple of years before, told everyone, "I think we've only gotten part of this out in the open. I was raised to think that coloreds—as we always called them— were to keep their place, and that blacks and whites shouldn't go to the same church. A lot of us still have some of that in us. We're trying to get rid of it, but change comes slow. All the same, I do know this: I was raised wrong. I'm trying to change. I hope the Struthers understand that those things don't always come easy for some of us."

At the end, Brother Giles stood and said, "I think maybe I've been the biggest problem for the Struthers. I wanted them to know I wasn't a bigot. But bigotry goes way back, runs deep in many of us, and the fact is, I just haven't learned to be really comfortable around blacks. That's my problem, and I'm sorry for it, but I have the feeling that we've all come a long way today. We're a people who ought to hate prejudice; we've experienced too much of it in our own history. Everyone of us knows what it's like to be made to feel strange just because we're Mormons.

"While I'm up here, I'd also like to thank Brother Ladd. He helped us see something, and I think we can take it from there. I want to thank Lucky too. He tried to show me the same thing the other night, and I was just too thick-headed to see it."

After the closing hymn and prayer, Brother Giles came down from the pulpit and shook hands with Brother and Sister Struthers, even gave them each a little hug. Others did the same. Lucky figured they were probably still overdoing it in some ways, but at least they seemed to understand now.

Malcolm cleared out as quickly as he could. Lucky thought he knew how Malcolm felt. No matter what the people had been saying, he still felt uncomfortable. And he sure didn't want to get himself hugged.

Lucky hurried out to the foyer, and then on outside. He found Malcolm out front. Yet when he faced Malcolm, he didn't know what to say.

"So are you guys leaving right away or what?" Malcolm asked.

"Dad doesn't know exactly. He's almost finished here, but he doesn't have another assignment yet."

"So you don't know where you'll be going?"

"Not yet."

"Maybe you'll get to play another game. Maybe you can still get a touchdown."

"Yeah. I'd like to do that. Or just knock down a few more guys." Lucky grinned.

Malcolm laughed, but not for long. "The coach thinks I'm a good player, but he never said about me what he said about you."

"I know. But I don't think he's right. I'm not tough. I'm just stubborn."

"Dad always says I'm stubborn. Maybe we're sort of alike."

Lucky wanted to think so, but he didn't say anything. In fact, neither boy could even stand to look at the other.

Malcolm finally got up the nerve to say it: "I wish you guys were going to stay around here longer."

"Yeah," Lucky said. "Me too. I didn't think I'd ever say that, but now it would be nice."

Once again, neither could come up with anything to say, and they looked away from each other. But Lucky did have one other thing on his mind. "Malcolm, if you told the guys to lay off Sharon, I think they'd do it."

Malcolm nodded, then said softly, "Yeah. Okay."

CHAPTER 12

Lucky went to practice on Tuesday. He hoped that he would still be around on Saturday. But on Wednesday, his dad came home and said that they were leaving Friday morning. They were heading to West Yellowstone, Montana.

On Thursday morning, he saw Sharon sitting in her usual place on the monkey bars. The night before, he and Dad had gone out with the crew from the church to the Talbot's house. The family had cleared away the old structure down to the floors. The men from the church had built the outside walls and raised them, then set the trusses for the roof. They accomplished a lot in one evening, more than Mr. Talbot and his sons could have done in a week. Sharon, however, hadn't been there, and she still didn't know Lucky was leaving.

"Sharon, we got word," Lucky said. "We're leaving Friday morning."

Lucky saw that she was taken by surprise. She didn't say so, though. She only asked, "Where you going?"

"Out by Yellowstone Park. Clear out in Montana."

"What's Yellowstone Park?"

"Haven't you heard of it? It's where Old Faithful is—the big geyser—and all the hot pots, and wild animals and all that stuff."

"What's a geyser?"

"It's a place where hot water shoots up in the air. Old Faithful goes up as high as a skyscraper. I saw it back a couple of years ago. It's really something."

Sharon nodded. "I'd like to see that. I'd like to see a skyscraper too. I just seen 'em on TV."

"Maybe your family could take a trip sometime. At least to New Orleans, or somewhere like that."

"Yeah, right."

"Don't you think you could?"

"We're not rich like you, Lucky. My daddy has an old truck, but we don't have nothin' we could take a trip in."

"I'm not rich. My dad just does work that makes him have to travel a lot."

"You're perty rich," Sharon said.

Lucky supposed that was so, by Sharon's standards. He didn't know what else to say.

"It's not good to move so much. You shouldn't have to do that."

"Well, I don't know. Dad says we're lucky. We get to see a lot of different places. I guess we learn a lot of stuff that way."

"You should've stayed here longer."

Lucky knew Sharon was trying to say something, though he didn't dare show her that he understood. "Well, Sharon, I think some things are going to change in the next couple of years. Everyone will grow a lot. Most everyone will be tall. You won't feel so different then."

"Maybe I can make friends with someone."

"Yeah, I'm sure you can. Are you going to try?"

"I already did."

"Did you? Who was it? One of the girls?"

"No."

"Who was it?"

Sharon looked down at her arms, resting on a bar in front of her. She couldn't say it, but Lucky suddenly realized she meant him. "My ma said that if I made friends with one, I can make friends with another."

"That's right. That's exactly right."

Sharon nodded, confidently.

"Hey, do you want to walk around a little?"

Sharon laughed and looked over at the boys playing touch football. She thought about it a bit, then said, "Naw. Once was enough."

"I hope you didn't feel bad about what happened."

Sharon looked surprised. She shook her head. "You stood up for me, Lucky. No one ever done that before."

Lucky nodded. "Sharon, did you know that a lot of the prettiest women in the world are tall? Models are almost all tall and thin. That's supposed to be the best way to look."

"Are you sure?" Sharon asked.

"Yeah, I'm sure. You're pretty now. Just think how beautiful you're going to be."

"I ain't perty, Lucky. Don't say that."

"Yeah, you are. Didn't you know that?"

She shook her head.

"Well, you are. Especially when you smile. You have dimples."

Sharon looked straight at the ground, and her face and neck turned scarlet. Quite some time passed before she said, "Don't say nothin' like that again, all right?"

"Why not? It's true."

"Jist don't say it, all right?"

"Okay. I won't. If you'll walk with me again."

"No. I don't want to do that neither." She still didn't look at him. "But if you could send me a postcard with a picture on it of that place, I'd like that."

"Okay. I'll tell you what. I'll send you one from every place I go. All over the whole country."

She looked up, and she smiled, dimples and all. "That'd be nice," she said. Then she added quickly, "But don't start thinkin' I'm your girlfriend."

"I won't. Don't worry." Lucky laughed, and then so did Sharon. She looked very nice.

Right after school, Lucky decided he'd go to practice that day even though he wouldn't be around for another game. Since his dad had finished up his work, he was in the RV when Lucky got home.

"You sure you want to do that?" his father asked. "You're going to have to sit for a long time while we're driving clear out west." He laughed enough to shake the walls.

Lucky replied that he needed to learn all he could. After all, he might be playing tackle football next year. "I sure hope I start to grow by then."

"Well, yeah. But you're lucky you didn't grow

early. If you'd done that, you would've missed out on all the stuff you've learned by being small."

"Yeah, right, Dad. I'm also lucky I have ugly teeth and big braces too."

"Well, sure. That's kind of obvious, isn't it? When you're a handsome guy like me someday, you won't be stuck up. You'll remember what it was like to have guys tease you about your teeth. Now me, I didn't have that advantage, and I'm afraid I'm a little vain about my good looks." He almost cracked the windows with his bellow.

"Okay, Dad. I get the idea. I'm going to go to practice and try to break my nose and knock a couple of teeth out, and maybe bust a leg. All that kind of stuff is lucky, according to you."

"True," his father said. "All the same, be careful. All right?"

"I'm always careful, Dad," Lucky said and laughed.

About an hour later, he showed up at the park for practice. He did all the regular drills and eventually got some playing time in the scrimmage. It didn't take him long to realize, however, that the rushers on his own team's defense had decided he'd taken enough. Most of the guys were treating him differently since Malcolm had changed his attitude — or maybe it was since the coach had said how tough he was. Either way, Lucky didn't like it. It was okay that they'd stopped their teasing, but he didn't want them to go soft on him.

"Coach," Lucky yelled. "We got a bunch of wimps on defense today. They aren't rushing hard. I think they're afraid of me."

Lucky saw Malcolm shake his head and laugh, as if to say, "The guy never learns."

"Come on!" Coach Denton yelled. "Give Lucky all he can handle. Out west, he might end up playing against some real men, not a bunch of pansies like you guys."

"That's right," Lucky said. "Let's see someone try to get past me."

So they lined up for a pass play, and this time the defensive line rushed hard. Big Carl struggled his way past a blocking lineman and charged toward Lucky. Lucky took him to the outside with his shoulder. He got knocked down hard but kept Carl from getting inside for a few seconds.

When he rolled over on the grass and looked behind him, he saw Malcolm running for his life and then losing his flag. The coach blew the whistle, and Malcolm got his flag back and attached it as he walked back. "You asked for it," he said to Lucky.

"Hey, I did my job. I blocked the guy outside.

If you'd stepped up into the pocket, the way you're supposed to, you would have gotten the pass off."

"What're you talking about? If I'd stepped up, he would've come right over the top of you. That's why I gave ground."

"No, no," Coach Denton said. "Lucky's right. He took the man outside, just the way I've been showing him. You're supposed to step up. I've been telling you that all year."

Malcolm looked at the coach, then at Lucky, and then back again at the coach. He wanted to argue; Lucky could see that. But he didn't. "Okay," he said. "I'll try to do that. Let's try another play."

"Good," the coach said. He nodded at Malcolm.

The guys started to huddle up. "Coach," Lucky said, "do you mind if I step out for a minute?"

"Why?"

Lucky took a deep breath. "That shoulder—the one I hit Carl with—it hurts all the way down to my knee."

"Are you okay? You didn't break anything, did you?"

"I don't think so."

The coach walked over and felt his shoulder, then rotated the arm. "It's not broken or out of socket," he said. "You must have just banged it good. Why don't you take a rest."

Lucky walked slowly away, over to where some of the substitute players stood. He really hurt bad. He slumped to his knees and held his shoulder. After a moment, though, he realized he didn't hear anything going on. He looked up. Everyone had stopped. Lucky looked around, saw that everyone seemed to be waiting. Even the coach was watching. Then Lucky thought he knew. He used his good arm to help himself and stood up. Coach Denton said, "Atta boy, Lucky."

Malcolm nodded: one solemn signal that said plenty.

Then the guys continued with their practice. Lucky's shoulder still hurt pretty bad, but he figured he was actually lucky. At least he had hurt a part of him he didn't have to sit on all the way to Montana.

About the Author

"Before I start a novel, I brainstorm," Dean Hughes says. "Then I work out an outline. I write many drafts of the book, sometimes nine or ten, before I'm satisfied. After teaching at the university level for eight years, I left to try writing full time. I've kept at it, and I'm pleased to say that I've been able to write over thirty books.

"I love to read children's books — every kind of book: fantasy, real life, mystery, history, science, biographies, and so on. I read all the time.

"The idea for the Lucky books came from Jim Metz's 1986–87 fourth-grade class. All the students helped me develop the idea for the main character and Lucky's family situation.

"I do some of my writing while I run. Running is one of my favorite pastimes. I even ran in the Deseret News Marathon in Salt Lake City once. While I jog, I process my writing ideas, working out problems and things like dialogue in my mind. I also like skiing, which may be why several of my books include skiing and snow. Golfing is fun, too.

"My wife, Kathy, and I live in Provo, Utah. We have three children high-school age and older: Tom, Amy, and Rob. I could talk all day about how wonderful they are, but this page is supposed to be about me, so I'll stop."

READ ON WITH THESE DESERET BOOK TITLES

	Order #	Price
__ **Show Me Your Rocky Mountains**		
Thelma Hatch Wyss 1769026		$4.95
__ **Saddle Shoe Blues**		
Carroll Hoefling Morris. .1320690		$9.95
__ **The Magic Garden . . . and Other Stories**		
Greg Larson. 1539751		$7.95
__ **The Miracle of Miss Willie**		
Alma J. Yates. 1443198		$4.95
__ **A Child's Story of the Book of Mormon** (4 vols. in 1)		
Deta Petersen Nealey. 1386778		$12.95
__ **If You Were a Boy in the Time of the Nephites**		
Pat Bagley. 1796265		$4.95
__ **If You Were a Girl in the Time of the Nephites**		
Pat Bagley. 1796247		$4.95

Look for these wherever Deseret Book publications are sold.

Or send check or money order to:

DESERET BOOK DIRECT
P.O. Box 30178
Salt Lake City, UT 84130-9952

Please send me the books I have checked above.

Total Merchandise	$_____
Sales Tax (if applicable)	$_____

Utah residents add 6 1/4%; Idaho residents
add 5%; California residents add 6 1/4%; Arizona
residents add 6 1/2%.

Shipping & Handling	$ 2.50
TOTAL (U.S. dollars only)	$_____

Prices are subject to change.

Name_____

Address_____

City_____ State_____ Zip Code_____

MORE OUTSTANDING BOOKS FROM DEAN HUGHES

	Order #	Price
__ Lucky's Crash Landing	1635490	$4.95
__ Lucky's Gold Mine	1912830	$4.95
__ Under the Same Stars	1592249	$4.95
__ Cornbread and Prayer	1524205	$8.95
__ Brothers	1769008	$4.95
__ The Mormon Church, a Basic History	1074095	$10.95

WATCH FOR THESE BOOKS FROM CINNAMON TREE

Enchantress of Crumbledown, by Donald R. Marshall

The Lord Needed a Prophet, by Susan Arrington Madsen

Look for these wherever Deseret Book publications are sold.

Or send check or money order to:

DESERET BOOK DIRECT
P.O. Box 30178
Salt Lake City, UT 84130-9952

Please send me the books I have checked above.

Total Merchandise	$_____
Sales Tax (if applicable)	$_____

Utah residents add 6 1/4%; Idaho residents add 5%; California residents add 6 1/4%; Arizona residents add 6 1/2%.

Shipping & Handling	$____2.50____
TOTAL (U.S. dollars only)	$_____

Prices are subject to change.

Name_____

Address_____

City_____ State_____ Zip Code_____